School Times

Ruskin Bond is known for his signature simplistic and witty writing style. He is the author of several bestselling short stories, novellas, collections, essays and children's books; and has contributed a number of poems and articles to various magazines and anthologies. At the age of twenty-three, he won the prestigious John Llewellyn Rhys Prize for his first novel, *The Room on the Roof*. He was also the recipient of the Padma Shri in 1999, Lifetime Achievement Award by the Delhi Government in 2012, and the Padma Bhushan in 2014.

Born in 1934, Ruskin Bond grew up in Jamnagar, Shimla, New Delhi and Dehradun. Apart from three years in the UK, he has spent all his life in India, and now lives in Landour, Mussoorie, with his adopted family.

RUSKIN BOND
School Times

RUPA

Published by
Rupa Publications India Pvt. Ltd 2010
7/16, Ansari Road, Daryaganj
New Delhi 110002

Sales centres:
Allahabad Bengaluru Chennai
Hyderabad Jaipur Kathmandu
Kolkata Mumbai

Selection copyright © Ruskin Bond 2010

Copyright of individual stories remain with the individual authors

This is a work of fiction. Names, characters, places and incidents
are either the product of the author's imagination or are used fictitiously,
and any resemblance to any actual persons, living or dead, events or
locales is entirely coincidental.

All rights reserved.
No part of this publication may be reproduced, transmitted, or
stored in a retrieval system, in any form or by any means, electronic,
mechanical, photocopying, recording or otherwise, without
the prior permission of the publisher.

ISBN: 978-81-291-4177-4

Ninth impression 2018

15 14 13 12 11 10 9

Typeset by Mindways Design, New Delhi

This book is sold subject to the condition that it shall not, by way
of trade or otherwise, be lent, resold, hired out, or otherwise circulated,
without the publisher's prior consent, in any form of binding or cover
other than that in which it is published.

Table of Contents

The Four Feathers 1
Ruskin Bond

Frank Fairleigh Sees the Macintosh Wonder,
and Rides Mad Bess 6
Francis Edward Smedley

A Fest of the Guinea-pigs and Tadpoles at St. Dominc's 20
Talbot Baines Reed

The Last Lesson 27
Alphonse Daudet

Schooldays: Raising the Wind 32
Gilbert Harding

My Grandmother and the Dirty English 38
Aubrey Menen

Prep School 48
Lord Berners

A Pair of Steel Spectacles 54
Richard Church

The Phantom Ship Steered by a Dead Man's Hand 59
Matthew Henry Barker

School Times

What Happened to a Father Who Became a Schoolboy 64
   F. Anstey

Nino Diablo 80
   W.H. Hudson

Undershorts and Roses 101
   Muzaffer Izgu

Til Eulenspiegel's Merry Pranks 109

Ullie's Dreams 114
   Heisel Anne Allison

Dreams of Elephants 119
   Thomas Palakeel

The Mountain 124
   Charles Mungoshi

Snails 132
   Dibakar Barua

Charge! 141
   Stephen Crane

Boy Among the Writers 152
   David Garnett

The Old Jug-Dodge has an Unexpected Victim 162
   Talbot Baines Reed

Getting Granny's Glasses 167
   Ruskin Bond

The Four Feathers

Ruskin Bond

OUR SCHOOL DORMITORY WAS A very long room with about thirty beds, fifteen on either side of the room. This was good for pillow fights. Class V would take on class VII (the two senior classes in our Prep-school) and there would be plenty of space for leaping, struggling small boys, pillows flying, feathers flying, until there was a cry of 'Here comes Fishy!' or 'Here comes Oily!' and either Mr Fisher, the headmaster, or Mr Oliver, the senior master, would come striding in, cane in hand, to put an end to the general mayhem. Pillow fights were allowed, up to a point; nobody got hurt. But parents sometimes complained if, at the end of the term, a boy came home with a pillow devoid of cotton-wool or feathers.

In that last year at Prep-school in Simla, there were four of us who were close friends — Bimal, whose home was in Bombay; Riaz, who came from Lahore; Brian, who hailed from Vellore; and your narrator, who lived wherever his father (then in the Air Force) was posted.

We called ourselves 'four feathers' — the feathers signifying that we were companions in adventure, comrades in arms, knights of the round table, etc. Bimal adopted a peacock's feather as his emblem; he was always a bit showy. Riaz chose a falcon's feather — although we couldn't find one. Brian and I were at first offered crows or *murghi* feathers, but we protested vigorously and threatened a walk-out. Finally, I settled for a parrot's feather (taken from Mr Fisher's pet parrot), and Brian found a woodpecker's, which suited him, as he was always knocking things about.

Bimal was all thin legs and arms, so light and frisky that at times he seemed to be walking on air. We called him 'Bambi', after the delicate little deer in the Disney Film. Riaz, on the other hand, was a sturdy boy, good at games but not very studious; but always good-natured, always smiling. Brian was a dark, good-looking boy from the south; he was just a little spoilt — hated being given out in a cricket match and would refuse to leave the crease! — but he was affectionate and a loyal friend. I was the 'scribe' — good at inventing stories in order to get out of scrapes — but hopeless at sums, my highest marks being 22 out of 100.

On Sunday afternoons, when there were no classes or organized games, we were allowed to roam about on the hillside below the school. The four feathers would laze about on the short summer grass, sharing the occasional food parcel from home, reading comics (sometimes a book), and making plans for the long winter holidays. My father, who collected everything from stamps to sea-shells to butterflies, had given me a butterfly-net and urged me to try and catch a rare species which, he said, was found only near Chotta Simla. He described it as a large purple butterfly with yellow and black borders on its wings. A 'Purple Emperor', I think it was called. As I wasn't very good at identifying butterflies, I would chase anything that happened to flit across the school grounds, usually ending up with common 'red admirals', 'clouded yellows', or 'cabbage whites'. But that 'Purple Emperor' — that rare specimen being sought by collectors the world over — proved elusive. I would have to seek my fortune in some other line of endeavour.

One day, scrambling about among the rocks and thorny bushes below the school, I almost fell over a small bundle lying in the shade of a young spruce tree. On taking a closer look, I discovered that the bundle was really a baby, wrapped up in a tattered old blanket.

The Four Feathers

'Feathers, feathers!' I called, 'come here and look. A baby's been left here!'

The feathers joined me, and we all stared down at the infant, who was fast asleep.

'Who would leave a baby on the hillside?' asked Bimal of no one in particular.

'Someone who doesn't want it,' said Brian.

'And hoped some good people would come along and keep it,' said Riaz.

'A panther might have come along instead,' I said. 'Can't leave it here.'

'Well, we'll just have to adopt it,' said Bimal. 'We can't adopt a baby,' said Brian.

'Why not?'

'We have to be married.'

'We don't.'

'Not us, you dope. The grown-ups who adopt babies.'

'Well, we can't just leave it here for grown-ups to come along,' I said.

'We don't even know if it's a boy or a girl,' said Riaz.

'Makes no difference. A baby's a baby. Let's take it back to school.'

'And keep it in the dormitory?'

'Of course not. Who's going to feed it? Babies need milk. We'll hand it over to Mrs Fisher. She doesn't have a baby.'

'Maybe she doesn't want one. Look, it's beginning to cry. Let's hurry!'

Riaz picked up the wide-awake and crying baby and gave it to Bimal who gave it to Brian who gave it to me. The four feathers marched up the hill to school with a very noisy baby.

'Now it has done potty in the blanket,' I complained, 'and some of it is on my shirt.'

'Never mind,' said Bimal. 'It's in a good cause. You're a Boy scout, remember. You're supposed to help people in distress.'

The headmaster and his wife were in their drawing-room, enjoying their afternoon tea and cakes. We trudged in, and Bimal announced, 'We've got something for Mrs Fisher.'

Mrs Fisher took a look at the bundle in my arms and let out a shriek. 'What have you brought here, Bond?'

'A baby ma'am. I think it's a girl. Do you want to adopt it?'

Mrs Fisher threw up her arms in consternation, and turned to her husband. 'What are we to do, Frank? These boys are impossible. They've picked up someone's child!'

'We'll have to inform the police,' said Mr Fisher, reaching for the telephone, 'we can't have lost babies in the school.'

Just then there was a commotion outside, and a wild-eyed woman, her clothes disheveled, entered at the front door accompanied by several men-folk from one of the villages. She ran towards us, crying out, 'My baby, my baby! *Mera bachcha!* You've stolen my baby!'

'We found it on the hillside,' I stammered.

'That's right,' said Brian. 'Finders keepers!'

'Quiet, Adams,' said Mr Fisher, holding up his hand for order and addressing the villagers in a friendly manner. 'These boys found the baby alone on the hillside and brought it here before—before—'

'Before the hyaenas got it,' I put in.

'Quite right, Bond. And why did you leave your child alone?' he asked the woman.

'I put her down for five minutes so that I could climb the plum tree and collect the plums. When I came down, the baby had gone! But I could hear it crying up on the hill. I called the men-folk and we came here looking for it.'

'Well, here's your baby,' I said, thrusting it into her arms. By then I was glad to be rid of it! 'Look after it properly in future.'

'Kidnapper!' she screamed at me.

The Four Feathers

Mr Fisher succeeded in mollifying the villagers. 'These boys are good scouts,' he told them. 'It's their business to help people.'

'Scout Laws Number Three, Sir,' I added. 'To be useful and helpful.'

And then the headmaster turned the tables on the villagers. 'By the way, these plum trees belong to the school. So do the peaches and apricots. Now I know why they've been disappearing so fast!'

The villagers, a little chastened, went their way. Mr Fisher reached for his cane. From the way he fondled it I knew he was itching to use it on our bottoms.

'No, Frank,' said Mrs Fisher, intervening on our behalf. 'It was really very sweet of them to look after that baby. And look at Bond — he's got baby-goo all over his clothes.'

'So he has. Go and take a bath, all of you. And what are you grinning about, Bond?' asked Mr Fisher.

'Scout Law Number Eight, Sir. A scout smiles and whistles under all difficulties.'

And so ended the first adventure of the four feathers.

Frank Fairleigh Sees the Macintosh Wonder, and Rides Mad Bess

Francis Edward Smedley

Francis Edward Smedley, the novelist, explaining how he came to write Frank Fairleigh, says 'it struck me that, while volume after volume had been devoted to "Schoolboy Days", and "College Life", the mysteries of that paradise of public-school-fearing mammas — a Private Tutor's — yet continued unrevealed.' And so, he resolved 'to enlighten these tender parents as to the precise nature of the rosebud into which they were so anxious to transplant their darlings.' Here then is a picture of a 'rosebud' of the early nineteenth century. Many of the incidents of Frank Fairleigh were based on the author's actual experiences. The story of the Macintosh has some historical interest. That useful garment was the result of an invention of Charles Macintosh, a Scottish chemist, who in 1823 took out a patent for his water-proof or 'mackintosh' clot: here Frank Fairleigh sees it for the first time.

ON RETURNING TO THE PUPILS' room, Lawless commenced (to my great delight, as I thereby enjoyed a complete immunity from his somewhat troublesome attentions) a full, true, and particular account of the pigeon-match, in which his friend Clayton had, with unrivalled skill, slain a sufficient number of victims to furnish forth pies for the supply of the whole mess during the ensuing fortnight. At length, however, all was said that could be said, even upon this interesting subject, and the narrator, casting his

Frank Fairleigh Sees the Macintosh Wonder, and Rides Mad Bess

eyes around in search of wherewithal to amuse himself, changed to espy my new writing-desk, a parting gift from my little sister Fanny who, with the self-denial of true affection, had saved up her pocket-money during many previous months, in order to provide funds for this munificent present.

'Pinafore, is that desk yours?' demanded Lawless.

Not much admiring the sobriquet by which he chose to address me, I did not feel myself called upon to reply.

'Are you deaf, stupid? Don't you hear me speaking to you? Where did you get that writing-desk?'

Still I did not answer.

'Sulky, eh? I shall have to lick him before long, I see. Here you, what's your name? Fairleigh, did your grandmother give you that writing-desk?'

'No,' I replied, 'my sister Fanny gave it to me the day before I left home.'

'Oh, you have got sister Fanny, have you? How old is she, and what is she like?'

'She is just thirteen, and she has got the dearest little face in the world,' I answered, earnestly, as the recollection of her bright blue eyes and sunny smile came across me.

'How interesting!' sighed Coleman; 'it quite makes my heart beat; you could not send for her, could you?'

'And she gave you that desk, did she? How very kind of her!' resumed Lawless, putting the poker in the fire.

'Yes, was it not?' I said eagerly. 'I would not have any harm happen to it for more than I can tell.'

'So, I suppose,' replied Lawless, still, devoting himself to the poker, which was rapidly becoming red-hot. 'Have you ever!' continued he, 'seen this new way they have of ornamenting things? Encaustic work, I think they call it; it's done by the application of heat, you know'

School Times

'I never even heard of it,' I said.

'Ah! I thought not,' enjoined Lawless. 'Well, as I happen to understand the process, I'll condescend to enlighten your ignorance. Mullins, give me that desk.'

My design was, however, frustrated by Cumberland and Lawless, who, both throwing themselves upon me at the same moment, succeeded, despite my struggles, in forcing me into a chair, where they held me, while Mullins, by their direction, with the aid of sundry neck cloths, braces, etc., tied my hand and foot; Coleman, who attempted to interfere in my behalf, receiving a push which sent him reeling across the room, and a hint that if he did not mind his own business he would be served in the same manner.

Having thus effectually placed me *horse de combat*, Lawless took possession of my poor writing-desk, and commenced tracing on the top thereof, with the red-hot poker, what he was pleased to term a 'design from the antique,' which consisted of a spirited outline of that riddle-loving female, the Sphinx, as she appeared when dressed in top-boots and a wide-awake, and regaling herself with a choice cigar! He was giving the finishing touch to a large pair of moustaches, with which he had embellished her countenance, and which he declared was the only thing wanting to complete the likeness to an old aunt of Dr Mildman's, whom the pupils usually designated by the endearing appellation of 'Growler', when the door opened, and Thomas announced that 'Smithson' was waiting to see Mr Lawless.

'Oh yes; to be sure, let him come in; no, wait a minute. Here, you, Coleman and Mullins, untie Fairleigh; be quick! Confound that desk; how it smells of burning, and I have made my hands all black too. Well, Smithson, have you brought the things?'

The person to whom this query was addressed, was a young man, attired in the extreme of the fashion, who lounged into the room, with a 'quite at home' kind of air, and nodding familiarly all around, arranged his curls with a ring-adorned hand, as he replied in a drawling tone:

'Ya'as, Mr Lawless, we're all right — punctual to a moment — always ready "to come to time," as we say in the ring.'

'Who is he?' I whispered to Coleman.

'Who is he?' replied Coleman. 'Why the best fellow in the world, to be sure. Don't know Smithson, the prince of tailors, the tailor par excellence! I suppose you never heard of the Duke of Wellington, have you?'

I replied humbly, that I believed I had heard the name of that illustrious individual mentioned in connection with Waterloo and the Peninsula — and that I was accustomed to regard him as the first man of the age.

'Aye, well then, Smithson is the second; though I really don't know whether he is not quite as great in his way as Wellington, upon my honour. The last pair of trousers he made for Lawless were something sublime, too good for this wicked world, a great deal.'

During this brief conversation, Smithson had been engaged in extricating a somewhat voluminous garment from the interior of a blue bag, which a boy, who accompanied him, had just placed inside the study-door.

'There, this is the new invention I told you about; a man named Macintosh hit upon it. Now, with this coat on, you might stand under a water-fall without getting even damp. Try it on, Mr Lawless; just the thing, eh, gents?'

Our curiosity being roused by this panegyric, we gathered around Lawless to examine the garment which had called it forth. Such of my readers as recollect the first introduction of Macintoshes, will doubtless remember that the earlier specimens of the race differed very materially in form from those which are in use at the present day. The one we were now inspecting was of a whity-brown colour, and though it had sleeves like a coat, hung in straight folds from the waist to the ankles, somewhat after the fashion of a carter's frock, having huge pockets at sides, and fastening round the neck with a hook and eye.

'How does it do?' asked Lawless, screwing himself around in an insane effort to look at the small of his own back, a thing a man is certain to attempt when trying on a coat. 'It does not make a fellow look like a guy, does it?'

'No, I rather admire the sort of thing,' said Cumberland.

A jolly dodge for a shower of rain, and no mistake,' said Coleman.

'It is deucedly fashionable really, said Smithson, 'this one of yours, and one we made for Augustus Flareaway Lord Fitz scamper's son, the man in the Guards, you know, are the only two out yet.'

'I have just got it at the right time then,' said Lawless; 'I knew old Sam was going to town, so I settled to drive Clayton over to Woodend, in the tandem, tomorrow. The harriers meet there at eleven, and this will be very thing to hide the leathers, and tops and the green cut-away. I saw you at the match, by-the-by, Sithey this morning.'

'Ya'as, I was there. Did you see the thing I was on?'

'A bright bay, with a star on the forehead! A spicy looking nag enough — whose is it?'

'Why young Robarts, who came into a lot of tin the other day, has just bought it; Snaffles charged him ninety guineas for it.'

And what is it worth?' asked Lawless.

'Oh! He would not do a dirty thing by any gent I introduced,' replied Smithson. 'I took young Robarts there: he merely made his fair profit out of it; he gave forty pounds for it himself to the man who bred it, only the week before, to my certain knowledge: it's a very sweet thing, and would carry him well, but he's afraid to ride it; that's how I was on it today. I'm getting it steady for him.'

A thing it will take you some time to accomplish, eh? A mount like that is not to be had for nothing, every day, is it?'

'Ya'as, you're about right there, Mr Lawless; you're down to every move, I see, as usual. Any orders today, gents? Your two vests will be home tomorrow, Mr Coleman.'

'Here, Smithson, wait a moment,' said Cumberland, drawing him on one side, 'I was deucedly unlucky with the balls this morning,' continued he in a lower tone, 'can you let me have five and twenty pounds?'

'What you please, sir,' replied Smithson, bowing.

'On the old terms, I suppose?' observed Cumberland.

'All right,' answered Smithson. 'Stay, I can leave it with you now,' added he, drawing out a leather case; 'oblige me by writing your name here — thank you.'

So saying, he handed some bank-notes to Cumberland, carefully replaced the paper he had received from him in his pocket-book, and withdrew.

'Smithey was in great force tonight,' observed Lawless, as the door closed behind him — 'nicely they are bleeding that young ass Robarts among them — he has got into good hands to help him to get rid of his money, at all events. I don't believe Snaffles gave forty pounds for that bay horse; he has got a decided curb on the off hock, if I ever saw one, and I fancy he's a little touched in the wind, too; and there's another thing I should say—'

What other failing might be attributed to Mr Robarts' bay seed, we were, however, not destined to learn, as tea was at this moment announced. In due time followed evening prayers, after which we retired for the night. Being very sleepy, I threw off my clothes, and jumped hastily into bed, by which act I became painfully aware of the presence of what a surgeon would term 'certain foreign bodies' — i.e. not, as might be imagined, sundry French, German, and Italian corpses, but various hard substances, totally opposed to one's preconceived ideas of the component parts of a feather-bed. Sleep being out of the question on a couch so constituted, I immediately commenced an active search, in the course of which I succeeded in bringing to light two clothes-brushes, a boot-jack, a pair of spurs, Lemprier's Classical Dictionary, and a brick-bat. Having freed myself from these undesirable bedfellows, I soon fell asleep, and passed (as it seemed to me) the whole night in dreaming that I was a pigeon, or thereabouts, and that Smithson, mounted on the top-booted Sphinx, was inciting Lawless to shoot at me with a red-hot poker. . .

[Frank Fairleigh is instigated by the unscrupulous Cumberland to ride Mad Bess, a hired horse. Coleman, a less experienced rider, is on a fat cob – Punch:]

Out of consideration for the excitable disposition of Mad Bess, we took our way along the least bustling streets we could select; directing our course towards the outskirts of the town, behind which extended for some miles a portion of the range of hills known as the South Downs, over the smooth green turf of which we promised ourselves a canter. As we rode along, Coleman questioned me as to what could have passed while he was seeing Punch saddled, to make me determine to ride the chestnut mare, whose vicious disposition was, he informed me, so well-known that not only would no one ride her who could help it, but that Snaffles, who was most anxious to get rid of her, had not as yet been able to find a purchaser. In reply to this, I gave him a short account of what had occurred, adding more suspicion to the whole matter that had been arranged by Cumberland, in which notion he entirely agreed with me.

'I was afraid of something of this sort, when I said I was sorry you had made that remark about cheating to him this morning — you see, he would no doubt suppose you had heard the particulars

Frank Fairleigh Sees the Macintosh Wonder, and Rides Mad Bess

of his gambling affair, and meant to insult him by what you said, and he has done this out of revenge. Oh, how I wish we were safely at home again; shall we turn back now?'

'Not for the world,' I said. 'You will find, when you know me better, that when once I have undertaken a thing I will go through with it; difficulties only make me more determined.'

The road becoming uneven and full of ruts, we agreed to turn our horses' heads, and quit it for the more tempting pathway afforded by the green-sward. No sooner, however, did Punch feel the change from the hard road to the soft elastic footing of the turn, than he proceeded to demonstrate his happiness by slightly elevating his heels, and propping his head down between his forelegs, thereby jerking the rein loose in Coleman's hand; and, perceiving that his rider (who was fully employed in grasping the pommel of his saddle in order to preserve his seat) made no effort to check his vivacity, he indulged his high spirits still further by setting off at a brisk canter.

'Pull him in,' I cried, 'you'll have him run away with you; pull at him.'

Whether my advice was acted upon or not I was unable to observe, as my whole attention was demanded by Mad Bess, who appeared at length resolved to justify the propriety of her appellation. Holding her in by means of the snaffle alone had been quite as much as I had been able to accomplish during the last ten minutes, and this escapade on the part of Punch brought the matter to a crisis. I must either allow her to follow him, i.e. to run away, or use the curb to prevent it. Seating myself, therefore, as firmly as I could, and gripping the saddle tightly with my knees, I took up the curb rein, which till now had been hanging loosely on the mare's neck, and gradually tightened it. This did not, for a moment, seem to produce any effect, but as soon as I drew the rein sufficiently tight to check her speed, she stopped short, and shook her head angrily. I attempted gently to urge her on—not a step except backwards would she stir — at length in despair I touched her slightly with the spur, and then 'the fiend within her woke,' and proceeded to make up for lost time with a vengeance. The moment the mare felt the spur, she reared until she stood perfectly erect, and fought the air with her forelegs. Upon this I slackened the rain, and striking her over the ears with, my riding-whip, brought her down again; no sooner, however, had her forefeet touched the ground than she gave two or three violent plunges, which nearly succeeded in unseating me, jerked down her head so suddenly as to loosen the reins from my grasp, kicked viciously several times, and seizing the cheek of the bit between her teeth so as to render it utterly useless (evidently an old trick of hers), sprang forward at a wild gallop. The pace at which we were going soon brought us alongside of Punch, who, having thoroughly mastered his rider, considered it highly improper that any steed should imagine itself able to pass him, and therefore proceeded to emulate the pace of Mad Bess. Thereupon, a short but very spirited race ensued, the cob's pluck enabling him to keep neck to neck for a few yards; but the mare was going at racing speed, and the length of her stride soon began to tell; Punch, too, showed signs of having nearly had enough of it. I therefore shouted to Coleman, as we were leaving them: 'Keep his head up hill, and you'll be able to pull him in directly.' His answer was inaudible, but when I turned my head a few minutes later, I was glad to see that he had followed my advice with complete success. Punch was standing still, about half a mile off, while his rider was apparently watching my course with looks of horror.

All anxiety on his account being thus at an end, I proceeded to take as calm a view of my own situation as circumstances would allow, in order to decide on the best means of extricating myself therefrom. We had reached the top of the first range of hills I have described, and were now tearing at a fearful rate down the descent on the opposite side. It was clear that the mare could not keep up the pace at which she was going for any length of time: still she was in first-rate racing condition, not an ounce of superfluous flesh about her, and, though she must have gone more than two miles already, she appeared as fresh as when we started. I, therefore, cast my eyes around in search of some obstacle which might check her speed. The slope down which we were proceeding extended for about a mile before us, after which the ground again began to rise. In the valley between the two hills was a small piece of cultivated land, enclosed (as is usual in the district I am describing) within a low wall, built of flint-stones from the beach. Towards this I determined to guide the mare as well as I was able, in the hope that she would refuse the leap, in which case I imagined I might pull her in. The pace at which we were going soon brought us near the spot, when I was glad to perceive that the wall was a more formidable obstacle than I had at first imagined, being fully six feet high, with a ditch in front of it. I, therefore, selected a place where the ditch seemed widest, got her head up by sawing her mouth with the snaffle, and put her fairly at it. No sooner did she perceive the obstacles before her, than, slightly moderating her pace, she appeared to collect herself, gathered her legs well under her, and rushing forward, cleared wall, ditch, and at least seven feet of ground beyond, with a leap like a deer, alighting safely with me on her back on the opposite side, where she continued her course with unabated vigour.

We had crossed the field (a wheat stubble) ere I had recovered from my astonishment at finding myself safe, after such a leap as I had most assuredly never dreamt of taking. Fortunately, there was a low gate on the farther side, towards which I guided the mare, for though I could not check I was in some measureable to direct her course. This time, however, she either did not see the impediment in her way, or despised it, as without abating her speed, she literally rushed through the gate, snapping into shivers with her chest, the upper bar, which was luckily rotten, and clearing the lower ones in her stride. The blow, and the splintered wood flying about her ears, appeared to frighten her afresh, and she tore up the opposite ascent, which was longer and steeper than the last, like a mad creature. I was glad to perceive, however, that the pace at which she had come, and the distance (which must have been several miles), were beginning to tell — her glossy coat was stained with sweat and dust, while her breath, drawn with short and laboured sobs, her heaving flanks and the tremulous motion of her limbs, afforded convincing proofs that the struggle could not be protracted much longer. Still, she continued to hold the bit between her teeth as firmly as though it were in a vice, rendering any attempt to pull her in utterly futile. We had now reached the crest of the hill, when I was not best pleased to perceive that the descent on the other side was much more precipitous than any I had yet met with. I endeavoured, therefore, to pull her head around, thinking it would be best to try and retrace our steps, but I soon found that it was useless to attempt it. The mare had now become wholly unmanageable; I could not guide her in the slightest degree; and, though she was evidently getting more and more exhausted, she still continued to gallop madly forwards, as though some demon had taken possession of her, and was urging her on to our common destruction. As we proceeded down the hill, our speed increased due to the force of gravitation, till we actually seemed to fly — the wind appeared to shriek as it rushed past my ears, while, from the rapidity with which we were moving, the ground seemed to glide from under us, till my head reeled so giddily that I was afraid I should fall from the saddle.

We had proceeded about half way down the descent, when, on passing one or two stunted bushes which had concealed the ground beyond, I saw, oh, horror of horrors; what appeared to be the mouth of an old chalk-pit, stretching dark and unfathomable right across our path, about 300 yards before us. The mare perceived it but it was too late, she attempted to stop, but from the impetus with which she was going, was unable to do so. Another moment, and we shall be over the brink! With the energy of despair, I lifted her with the rein with both hands, and drove the spurs madly into her flanks; she rose to the leap, there was a bound! A sensation of flying through the air! A crash! And I found myself stretched in safety on the turf, beyond, and Mad Bess lying, panting, but uninjured beside me.

To spring upon my feet, and seize the bridle of the mare, who had also by this time recovered her footing, was the work of a moment. I then proceeded to look around, in order to gain a more clear idea of the situation in which I was placed, in the hope of discovering the easiest method of extricating myself from it. Close behind me lay the chalk-pit, and as I gazed down its rugged sides, overgrown with brambles and rank weeds, I shuddered to think of the probable fate from which I had been so almost miraculously preserved, and turned away with a heartfelt expression of thanksgiving to Him, who had mercifully decreed that the thread of my young life should not be snapped in so sudden and fearful a manner. Straight before me, the descent became almost suddenly precipitous, but a little to the right I perceived a sort of sheep-track, winding downwards round the side of the hill. It was a self-evident fact that this must lead somewhere, and, as all places were alike to me, so that they contained any human beings who were able and willing to direct me towards Helmstone, I determined to follow it. After walking about half a mile, Mad Bess (with her ears drooping, and her nose nearly touching the ground) following me as quietly as a dog, I was rejoiced by the sight of curling smoke, and on turning a corner, I came suddenly upon a little village green, around which some half dozen cottages were scattered at irregular distances. I directed my steps towards one of these, before which a crazy sign, rendered by age and exposure to the weather as delightfully vague and unintelligible as though it had come fresh from the brush of Turner himself, hung picturesquely from the branch of an old oak.

The sound of horse's feet attracted the attention of an elderly man, who appeared to combine in his single person the offices of ostler, waiter, and boots, and who, as soon as he became aware of my necessities, proceeded to fulfil the duties of these various situations with the greatest alacrity. First (as of the most importance in his eyes) he rubbed down Mad Bess, and administered some refreshment to her in the shape of hay and water; then he brought me a glass of ale, declaring it would do me good (in which, by the way, he was not far from right). He then brushed from my coat certain stains, which I had contracted in my fall, and finally told me my way to Helmstone. I now remounted Mad Bess, who, though much refreshed by the hay and water, still continued perfectly quiet and tractable; and setting off at a moderate trot, reached the town, after riding about eight miles, without any further adventure, in rather less than an hour.

As I entered the street in which Snaffles' stables were situated, I perceived Coleman and Lawless standing at the entrance of the yard, evidently awaiting my arrival. When I got near them, Coleman sprang eagerly forward to meet me, saying:

'How jolly glad I am to see you safe again, old fellow! I was so frightened about you. How did you manage to stop her?'

'Why, Fairleigh, I had no idea you were such a rider,' exclaimed Lawless. 'I made up my mind you would break your neck, and old Sam be minus a pupil, when I heard you were gone out on that mare. You have taken the devil out of her somehow, and no mistake; she's as quiet as a lamb,' added he, patting her.

'You were very near being right,' I replied, 'she did her best to break my neck and her own too, I can assure you.'

I then, proceeded to relate my adventures, to which both Lawless and Coleman listened with great attention; the former interrupting me every now and then with various expressions of commendation,

Frank Fairleigh Sees the Macintosh Wonder, and Rides Mad Bess

and when I had ended, he shook me warmly by the hand, saying:

'I give you great credit; you behaved in a very plucky manner all through; I didn't think you had it in you; 'pon my word, I didn't. I shall just tell Cumberland and Snaffles a bit of my mind, too.'

– Francis Edward Smedley: *Frank Fairleigh (1850).*

A Fest of the Guinea-pigs and Tadpoles at St. Dominc's

Talbot Baines Reed

'Tadpoles' and 'Guinea-pigs' were the names of two sets in the clannish Junior School of St. Dominic's. In the middle of their annual celebration, they attract the attention of the seniors, Oliver Greenfield and Horance Wraysford — two fine characters in The Fifth Form at St. Dominic's. This is the best-known book of that admirable boys' author Talbot Baines Reed, appeared (as did most of his tales) in B.O.P. — or the Boy's Own Paper of splendid memory.

JUST AT THAT MOMENT A terrific row came up from below.

'What's happening down there?'

'Only the Guinea-pigs and Tadpoles. By the way, said Wraysford, 'they've got a grand "supper", as they call it, on tonight to celebrate their cricket match. Suppose we go and see the fun?'

'All right!' said Oliver. 'Who won the match?'

'Why, what a question! Do you suppose a match between Guinea-pigs and Tadpoles ever came to an end? They had a free fight at the end of the first innings. The Tadpoles umpire gave one of his own men "not out" when he hit his wicket, and they made a personal question of it, and fell out. Your young brother, I hear, greatly distinguished himself in the argument.'

'Well, it doesn't seem to interfere with their spirits now, to judge by the row they are making. Just listen!'

By this time they had reached the door of the Fourth Junior

A Fest of the Guinea-pigs and Tadpoles at St. Dominc's

room, whence proceeded a noise such as one often hears in a certain popular department of the Zoological Gardens. Amid the tumult and hubbub, the two friends had not much difficulty in slipping in unobserved and seating themselves comfortably in an obscure corner of the festive apartment, behind a pyramid of piled-up chairs and forms.

The Junior 'cricket feast' was an institution in St. Dominic's, and was an occasion when anyone who had nerves to be excruciated or ear-drums to be broken took care to keep out of the way. In place of the usual desks and forms, a long table ran down the room, around which some fifty or sixty urchins sat, regaling themselves with what was left of a vast spread of plum-cake, buns, and ginger beer. How these banquets were provided was always a mystery to outsiders. Some said a levy of threepence a head was made; others said that every boy was bound in honour to contribute something eatable to the feast; and others averred that every boy had to bring his own bag and bottle, and no more. Be that as it might, the Guinea-pigs and Tadpoles at present assembled looked uncommonly tight about the jackets after it all, and not one had the appearance of actual starvation written on his lineaments.

The animal part of the feast, however, was now over, and the intellectual was beginning. The tremendous noise which had brought Oliver and Wraysford on to the scene had indeed been but the applause which followed the chairman's opening song — a musical effort which was imperatively encored by a large and enthusiastic audience.

The chairman, by the way, was no other than our friend Bramble, who by reason of seniority — he had been two years in the Fourth Junior, and showed no signs of rising higher all his life — claimed to preside on all such occasions. He sat up at the top end in stately glory, higher than the rest by the thickness of a Liddell and Scott, which was placed on his chair to lift him up to the required elevation,

School Times

blushingly receiving the applause with which his song was greeted, and modestly volunteering to sing it again if the fellows liked.

The fellows did like. Mr Bramble mounted once more on to the seat of his chair, and saying, 'Look out for the chorus!' began one of the time-honoured Dominican cricket songs. It consisted of about twelve verses altogether, but three will be quite enough for the reader.

'There was a little lad,
      (Well bowled!)
And a little bat he had;
      (Well bowled!)
He skipped up to the wicket,
And thought he'd play some cricket,
But he didn't for he was—
      Well bowled!

'He thought he'd make a score
      (So bold),
And lead off with a four
      (So bold);
So he walked out to a twister,
But somehow sort of missed her,
And she bailed him, for he was
      Too bold.

'Now all ye little boys
      (So bold),
Who like to make a noise
      (So bold),
Take warning by young Walker,
Keep your bat down to a yorker,
Or, don't you see? You'll be—
      Well bowled!'

A Fest of the Guinea-pigs and Tadpoles at St. Dominc's

The virtue of the pathetic ballad was in the chorus, which was usually not sung, but spoken, and so presented a noble opportunity for variety of tone and expression, which was greedily seized upon by the riotous young gentlemen into whose mouths it was entrusted. By the time the sad adventures of Master Walker had been rehearsed in all their twelve verses, the meeting was so hoarse that to the two elder boys it seemed as if the proceedings must necessarily come abruptly to a close for want of voice.

But no! If the meeting was for the moment incapable of song, speech was yet possible, and behold there arose Master Paul in his place to propose a toast.

Now Master Paul was a Guinea-pig, and accounted a mighty man in his tribe. Any one might have supposed that the purpose for which he had now risen was to propose in complimentary terms the health of his gallant opponents, the Tadpoles. This, however, was far from his intention. His modesty had another theme. 'Ladies and gentlemen,' he began. There were no ladies present, but that didn't matter. Tremendous cheers greeted this opening. 'You all know me; I am one of yourselves.' Paul had borrowed this expression from the speech of a radical orator, which had appeared recently in the papers. Everyone knew it was borrowed, for he had asked about twenty of his friends during the last week whether that wouldn't be 'a showy lead-off for his cricket feast jaw?'

The quotation was, however, now greeted as vociferously as if it had been strictly original, and shouts of 'so you are!' 'Bravo, Paul!' for a while drowned the orator's voice. When silence was restored his eloquence took a new and unexpected departure. 'Jemmy Welch, I'll punch your head when we get outside, see if I don't!' Jemmy Welch was a Guinea-pig who had just made a particularly good shot at the speaker's nose with a piece of plum-cake. 'Now, ladies and gentlemen, I shall detain you with a speech (loud cheers from all, and "Jolly good job!" from Bramble). I shall go on speaking just as long as I choose, Bramble, so now! (Cheers). I've as much right to speak as you have. (Applause). You're only a stuck-up duffer. (Terrific cheers, and a fight down at the end of the table). I beg to drink the health of the Guinea-pigs. (Loud Guinea-pig cheers). We licked the old Tadpoles in the match. ("No you didn't!" "That's a cram!" and groans from the Tadpoles). I say we did! Your umpire was a cheat — they always are! We beat you hollow, didn't we, Stee Greenfield?'

'Yes, rather!' shouted Stephen, snatching a piece of cake away from a Tadpole and shying it to a Guinea-pig.

'That's eight matches we've won,' proceeded Paul; 'and — all right, Spicer! I saw you do it this time! See if I don't pay you for it!' Whereat the speaker hurriedly quitted his seat and, amid howls and yells, proceeded to 'pay out' Spicer.

Meanwhile Stephen heard his name suddenly called upon for a song, an invitation he promptly obeyed. But as the clamour was at the time deafening, and the attention of the audience was wholly monopolized by the commercial transactions taking place between Paul and Spicer, the effect of the performance was somewhat lost. Oliver certainly did see his young brother mount up on the table, turn very red in the face, open his mouth and shut it, smile in one part, look sorrowful in another, and wave his hand above his head in another. But that was the only intimation he had of a musical performance proceeding. Words and tune were utterly inaudible by any except the single himself — even if he heard them.

This was getting monotonous, and the two visitors were thinking of withdrawing, when the door suddenly opened, and a dead silence prevailed. The newcomer was the dirtiest and most

A Fest of the Guinea-pigs and Tadpoles at St. Dominc's

ferocious-looking of all the boys in the lower school, who rushed into the room breathless, and in what would have been a white heat had his face been clean enough to show it. 'What do you think?' he gasped, catching hold of the back of a chair for support; 'Tony Pembury's kept me all this while brushing his clothes! I told him it was cricket feast, but he didn't care! What do you think of that? Of course, you've finished all the grub; I knew you would!'

This last plaintive wail of disappointment was drowned in the clamour of execration which greeted the boy's announcement. Lesser feuds were instantly forgotten in the presence of this great insult. The most sacred traditions of Guinea-pigs and Tadpoles were being trampled upon by the tyrants of the upper school! Not even on cricket feast night was a fag to be let off fagging!

It was enough! The last straw breaks the camel's back, and the young Dominicans had now reached the point of desperation.

It was long before silence enough could be restored, and then the redoubtable Spicer yelled out, 'Let's strike!'

The cry was taken up with yells of enthusiasm — 'Strike! No more fagging!'

'Any boy who fags after this,' screamed Bramble, 'will be cut dead! Those who promise hold up your hands — mind, it's a promise!'

There was no mistaking the temper of the meeting, every hand in the room was held up.

'Mind now, no giving in!' cried Paul. 'Let's stick all together. Greenfield senior shall kill me before I do anything more for him!'

'Poor fellow!' whispered Oliver, laughing; 'what a lot of martyrdoms he'll have to put up with!'

'And Pembury shall kill me,' squealed the last comer, who had comforted himself with several crusts of plum-cakes and the dregs of about a dozen bottles of ginger beer.

And every one protested their willingness to die in the good cause.

At this stage, Oliver and Wraysford withdrew unobserved. 'I'm afraid we've been eavesdropping,' said Oliver. Anyhow, I don't mean to take advantage of what I've heard.'

[The strike of the fags occurred towards the end of term. The 'Guinea-pig' and 'Tadpoles' cooled down in spirit during the holidays; and when the next term began, they returned to work just as if the mighty strike had never broken out. In short, 'everything was quite like old times' again.]

– Talbot Baines Reed: *The Fifth Form at St. Dominic's (1887)*

The Last Lesson

Alphonse Daudet

The short story as a literary form was particularly suited to the French literary genius, and Alphonse Daudet (1840—94) was one of its finest exponents.

STARTED FOR SCHOOL VERY LATE that morning and was in great dread of a scolding, especially because M. Hamel had said that he would question us on participles, and I did not know the first word about them. For a moment I thought of running away and spending the day out of doors. It was so warm, so bright! The birds were chirping at the edge of the woods; and in the open field, back of the saw-mill, the Prussian soldiers were drilling. It was all much more tempting than the rule for participles, but I had the strength to resist, and hurried off to school.

When I passed the town hall there was a crowd in front of the bulletin board. For the last two years all our bad news had come from there — the lost bat, ties, the draft, the orders of the commanding officer — and I thought to myself, without stopping:

'What can be the matter now?'

Then, as I hurried by as fast as I could go, the blacksmith, Wachter, who was there, with his apprentice, reading the bulletin, called after me:

'Don't go so fast, bub; you'll get to your school in plenty of time!'

I thought he was making fun of me, and I reached M. Hamel's little garden all out of breath.

School Times

Usually, when school began, there was a great bustle, which could be heard out in the street, the opening and closing of desks, lessons repeated in unison, very loud, with our hands over our ears to understand better, and the teacher's great ruler rapping on the table. But now it was all so still! I had counted on the commotion to get to my desk without being seen; but, of course, that day everything had to be as quiet as Sunday morning. Through the window I saw my classmates, already in their places, and M. Hamel walking up and down with his terrible iron ruler under his arm. I had to open the door and go in before everybody. You can imagine how I blushed and how frightened I was.

But nothing happened. M. Hamel saw me and said very kindly: 'Go to your place quickly, little Franz. We were beginning without you.'

I jumped over the bench and sat down at my desk. Not till then, when I had got a little over my fright, did I see that our teacher had on his beautiful green coat, his frilled shirt, and the little black silk cap, all embroidered, that he never wore except on inspection and prize days. Besides, the whole school seemed so strange and solemn. But the thing that surprised me most was to see, on the back benches that were always empty, the village people were sitting quietly like ourselves; old Hauser, with his three-cornered hat, the former mayor, the former postmaster, and several others besides. Everybody looked sad; and Hauser had brought an old primer, thumbed at the edges, and he held it open on his knees with his great spectacles lying across the pages.

While I was wondering about it all, M. Hamel mounted his chair, and, in the same grave and gentle tone which he had used to me, said:

'My children, this is the last lesson I shall give you. The order has come from Berlin to teach only German in the schools of Alsace and Lorraine. The new master will come tomorrow. This is your last

The Last Lesson

French lesson. I want you to be very attentive.'

What a thunderclap these words were to me!

Oh, the wretches; that was what they had put up at the town-hall!

My last French lesson! Why, I hardly knew how to write! I should never learn any more! I must stop there, then! Oh, how sorry I was for not learning my lessons, for seeking birds' eggs, or going sliding on the Saar! My books, that had seemed such a nuisance a while ago, so heavy to carry, my grammar, and my history of the saints, were old friends now that I couldn't give up. And M. Hamel, too; the idea that he was going away, that I should never see him again, made me forget all about his ruler and how cranky he was.

Poor man! It was in honor of this last lesson that he had put on his fine Sunday-clothes, and now I understood why the old men of the village were sitting there in the back of the room. It was because they were sorry, too, that they had not gone to school more. It was their way of thanking our master for his forty years of faithful service and of showing their respect for the country that was theirs no more.

While I was thinking of all this, I heard my name called. It was my turn to recite. What would I not have given to be able to say that dreadful rule for the participle all through, very loud and clear, and without one mistake? But I got mixed up on the first words and stood there, holding on to my desk, my heart beating, and not daring to look up. I heard M. Hamel say to me: 'I won't scold you, little Franz; you must feel bad enough. See how it is! Every day we have said to ourselves: "Bah! I've plenty of time. I'll learn it tomorrow." And now you see where we've come out. Ah, that's the great trouble with Alsace; she puts off learning till tomorrow. Now those fellows out there will have the right to say to you: "How is it; you pretend to be Frenchmen, and yet you can neither speak nor write your own language?" But you are not the worst, poor little Franz. We've all a great deal to reproach ourselves with.

School Times

'Your parents were not anxious enough to have you learn. They preferred to put you to work on a farm or at the mills, so as to have a little more money. And I? I've been to blame also. Have I not often sent you to water my flowers instead of asking you to learn your lessons? And when I wanted to go fishing, did I not just give you a holiday?'

Then, from one thing to another, M. Hamel went on to talk of the French language, saying that it was the most beautiful, language in the world — the clearest, the most logical; that we must guard it among us and never forget it, because when people are enslaved, as long as they hold fast to their language it is as if they had the key to their prison. Then he opened a grammar book and read our lesson. I was amazed to see how well I understood it. All he said seemed so easy, so easy! I think, too, that I had never listened so carefully, and that he had never explained everything with so much patience. It seemed almost as if the poor man wanted to give us all he knew before going away, and to put it all into our heads at one stroke.

After the grammar, we had a lesson in writing. That day, M. Hamel had new copies for us, written in a beautiful round hand: France, Alsace, France, Alsace. They looked like little flags floating everywhere in the schoolroom, hung from the rod at the top of our desks. You ought to have seen how everyone set to work, and how quiet it was! The only sound was the scratching of the pens over the paper. Once some beetles flew in; but nobody paid any attention to them, not even the littlest ones, who worked right on tracing their fish-hooks, as if that was French, too. On the roof the pigeons cooed very low, and I thought to myself:

'Will they make them sing in German, even the pigeons?'

Whenever I looked up from my writing, I saw M. Hamel sitting motionless in his chair and gazing first at one thing, then at another, as if he wanted to fix in his mind just how everything looked in that little schoolroom. Fancy! For forty years he had been there in the

The Last Lesson

same place, with his garden outside the window and his class in front of him, just like that. Only the desks and benches had been worn smooth; the walnut trees in the garden were taller, and the hop-vine that he had planted himself twined about the windows to the roof. How it must have broken his heart to leave it all, poor man; to hear his sister moving about in the room above, packing their trunks! For they must leave the country next day.

But he had the courage to hear every lesson to the very last. After the writing, we had a lesson in history, and then the babies chanted their ba, be, bi, bo, bu. Down there at the back of the room old Hauser had put on his spectacles and, holding his primer in both hands, spelled the letters with them. You could see that he, too, was crying; his voice trembled with emotion, and it was so funny to hear him that we all wanted to laugh and cry. Ah, how well I remember it, that last lesson!

All at once the church-clock struck twelve. Then, the Angelus. At the same moment the trumpets of the Prussians, returning from drill, sounded under our windows. M. Hamel stood up, very pale, in his chair. I never saw him look so tall.

'My friends,' said he, 'I—I—' But something choked him. He could not go on.

Then he turned to the blackboard, took a piece of chalk, and, bearing on with all his might, he wrote as large as he could:

'Vive La France!'

Then he stopped and leaned his head against the wall, and, without a word, he made a gesture to us with his hand: 'School is dismissed — you may go.'

Schooldays: Raising the Wind

Gilbert Harding

IN ORDER TO GET ME into Wolverhampton's Royal Orphanage, Mother had to write round to all the Patrons and subscribers of the School which, then, as still today, is 'entirely supported by voluntary contributions'. It was founded in 1850 when it was known as the Wolverhampton Orphan Asylum.

I was delighted when mother's first attempt was unsuccessful. We had gone to tea at the home of a local dentist whose son, Freddy Volpe, a lad about two years older to me, took me aside and warned me not to let myself be sent there. With great skill and vivid description he drew hideous pictures of what went on there and told me that I should hate the school as much as he did.

Then one dreadful afternoon my mother told me that I had 'got in'. I wept. I went to my room and cried myself to sleep. When, a few weeks later, I did have to leave home, I did so with tears and lamentation.

It was on 28 August 1916, that my mother took me in a smelly old horse-drawn cab from the Low Level Station to the Royal Orphanage. We arrived carrying a suitcase in which mother was to take back the clothes I was wearing. What is beyond my power of description is the dreadful feeling of finality, the terrifying and almost unbelievable sense of leaving behind forever the carefree days.

I was a very spoilt little boy badly behaved, selfish and liable to violent fits of temper if I did not get my own way quickly enough.

Schooldays: Raising the Wind

Now all I knew was that I was going to be separated from my mother, who had been my protector and shield, and that I was going to be locked up and thrust into a uniform which I thought was very silly, anyhow.

The newcomers were 'received' and examined by a Dr Dent, whom I liked at once, but under the eagle eye of the Matron, whom I felt I should never like. Then we were given our uniforms and I was horrified by the shirt and terrible broadcloth pants, and boots! Grotesquely clad, we were taken back to say goodbye. My mother was upset by the sight of me, but she was able to smile and tell me she had seen the dinner and that it 'looked very nice'.

Sometime later we new boys were taken to a room where, to my unspeakable shame, we all had to get into a big bath together under the supervision of a maid. This was the final humiliation.

Our life was highly institutional. Boys always wore the dreadful heavy boots which so depressed me on seeing them for the first time. We also wore brown stockings, moleskin, breeches, long blue coats and white bibs — just like Christ's Hospital but not so smart. The food was adequate, but quite disgusting.

Routine soon established its drably rigid pattern. We got up in the unheated dormitories at six-thirty, lined-up to go downstairs for a strip-wash in cold water (hot water was unheard of, except for the weekly bath) and then into school at seven-fifteen for three-quarters of an hour of 'prep' before breakfast.

There was never any doubt what breakfast would be. Sunday, Monday, Wednesday and Friday: bread and margarine, and occasionally jam or marmalade, with cocoa. Tuesday, Thursday and Saturday: porridge as well. Two bits of bread when there was porridge, four when there was not. And this delicious food was eaten off chipped enamel plates, the cocoa drunk from chipped enamel mugs. When our relatives sent us eggs we were allowed to put our names on them and have them cooked for us.

School Times

School began at nine and went on till twelve-fifteen. Then came lunch. There was never any doubt about that, either! Sunday: bully beef and beetroot with potatoes boiled in their skins (they were always boiled in their skins!), followed by steered prunes. Monday: mince, followed by rice pudding. Tuesday: bully beef followed by *'gobby'*, a kind of fruit pudding in which we found the oddest things from rats' tails and bits of string to fragments of sacking. Wednesday: fish (boiled cod) and potatoes; rice pudding. Thursday's dinner I have forgotten but I know it was something awful — probably 'stew'. Friday: a different kind of 'gobby' — a kind of meat pudding which consisted of a soggy crust and a lump of rainbow-coloured fat. No one ever ate all the lumps of fat.

One day, shortly after I arrived, the headmaster complained about waste. Now it was an understood thing that the bread plate was used for unwanted bits of fat, the plate being passed from boy to boy as and when he needed it. That day the headmaster chose to follow up his words by making a tour of the dining hall. Unfortunately, he saw this plate stacked with chewed fat which happened, at that moment, to be in front of me. He did not ask if it were mine. He simply ordered me to eat it up.

I looked at the messy pile with a nasty feeling beginning to churn up inside.

'Eat it up, boy!' the headmaster roared. 'We do not want any waste here.'

'But, sir, I didn't put any of that stuff on the plate,' I said.

'Eat it up,' the headmaster said, pushing my face towards the mess. So I had no alternative but to swallow the other boys' leavings, and promptly be sick on the spot.

Our routine continued with afternoon school between two and four o'clock, except on Wednesdays and Saturdays. Tea was at six

Schooldays: Raising the Wind

and always exactly the same as breakfast except for the porridge. No more was eaten between then and bed time except one dry biscuit, which was handed to us at eight-thirty. Wednesday and Saturday afternoons would be devoted to 'games'. There was an asphalt yard and a playroom and a covered playground. I didn't enjoy games very much, though later I did get around to running and once won the junior 220 yards, the prize for which was a small box camera.

We were always bathed in batches of twenty at a time in a great tub. After my initial humiliation and shock, I got accustomed to this but I never became reconciled to the state of the water which was not changed for each batch. If you were in the third batch, you had to push back a sea of scum as you went in.

We were astonishingly well taught. Indeed, there was little else to do except learn. The headmaster was one of the most remarkable men I have ever known. He was the Rev. Frank Lampitt, known as 'Dad'. Feared and hated by most of the boys, he loomed over our lives, a grim figure with a grey moustache stained by tobacco chewing and incessant smoking. When he spoke, tobacco juice would spray all over us.

I now realize what he was up against. His own salary was meagre. Not a single man on the staff had a degree. We were, remember, in the middle of the First World War and the maximum salary paid to the assistant masters was £70 a year. The only good masters were very young old boys' waiting for military call-up. Others came from the hedges by the look of them. Some drank, others were illiterate. But a few of them were able and efficient.

'Dad' Lampitt therefore took it upon himself — since he could get no master capable of doing it — to keep order unaided. He imposed what was virtually a reign of terror. He came round the dormitories to keep order as we got up and dressed. Then he would preside over

School Times

breakfast in the dining hall. Between rising and breakfast time he gave extra tuition in the big schoolroom to advanced scholars, then taught for every period, morning and afternoon. He would take his seat in the hall at lunch time and go on to teach all the afternoon; and then again during evening prep. Finally he would supervise the masters rounds of the dormitories. He was already a very tired man when I arrived at the school in 1916.

We did not have evening chapel in those days. Lampitt would conduct a service early in the afternoon, and instead of evening services he would read aloud to us from such books as Dombey and Son. Whenever anyone's attention began to wander, he would look up from his massive volume and roar at the culprit: 'Come out, you! You seem to forget that my spectacles reflect everything!'

I never did anything so exciting as to run away from school, though I often thought about it. The fate of those who tried was so awful that I always stayed out. Shortly before evening prep, some time during my first year at Wolverhampton, we were all ordered to assemble in a classroom. We filed in, wondering what catastrophe lay ahead. At last 'Dad' Lampitt stalked in, followed by two boys who had tried to run away. I think their names were Mayrick and Otty.

One after the other, the boys were soundly flogged until I was almost sick with shock and nausea. This dreadful spectacle checked me whenever my thoughts strayed toward the freedom of the outside world.

While I was never actually hungry, I was always ravenous for titbits; chocolate creams, buns, ginger pop. Mother used to send me pocket money to buy little extras, but one day Lampitt stopped that, telling her: 'He must accept only what is given to him at the school. The boy already has a tendency to show off.'

So I wrote to mother telling her that I had broken a window and needed five shillings to pay for its repair. This I duly received in the

Schooldays: Raising the Wind

post. But when I wrote and told her that I had lost a textbook and needed to replace it, mother had just planned to visit me at school and arrived to take me out to tea. Not having been informed that she was coming, I was scared when I was sent for to put my best coat on and report to the headmaster's study. I was relieved and overjoyed to find mother there, holding a promising looking suitcase.

'Your mother has come to take you to tea,' Lampitt said.

As we were about to leave, to my horror mother produced five separate shillings which she handed to the headmaster, saying: 'Here is the money for the textbook Gilbert lost.'

Lampitt said nothing.

That night, before he began one of his readings from Dickens, he said: 'Stand up, Harding, liar and thief! I keep my money in a cash box in the lower left hand drawer. The box is never locked. If you ever want money, you now know where to steal it — from me, not your mother.'

Lampitt then flung the five shillings at me, ordering me to pick them up. I refused.

'Pick it up!' he shouted.

I slunk from my desk and, on all fours, groped for the money.

'Now get out!' Lampitt thundered, when I had collected my pieces of silver. I did so, feeling as Judas Iscariot must have done before he strung himself up.

— From *Along My Line*

My Grandmother and the Dirty English

Aubrey Menen

My ANCESTORS ON MY MOTHER'S side wear brigands who infested a range of hills overlooking the Lake of Killarney, called Macgillicuddy's Reeks. Two things are known to have run in their blood — a tendency to end up on the gallows and an itch to harry the English. I have managed to eradicate the first.

My ancestors on my father's side are Nayars of Malabar, a tropical stretch of country in the south of India. In the days when Malabar was ruled by a king, they performed the rite of cutting him up with scimitars at the end of a stated period of years. After this they chose another ruler. In due course, he in his turn was ceremonially cut up by my ancestors, who chose another, and so on. They had no other democratic traits. They are to this day rigidly conscious of their class and strict in the observance of untouchability. They live by growing coconuts and grinding the faces of the poor, if by this it is understood that the operation takes place at the ritual distance of twenty feet from any member of my family.

My father, having run away from his family and come to England, married my mother. He was cut off with a rupee.

Shortly after I was born it became clear that both strains of my ancestry had taken part in shaping me. I had inherited from my Indian side a brown complexion; and I began to talk volubly at an early age.

My father doted on me, but he was aware that the future would hold problems. When he mentioned these to my mother, she, looking out of the window and seeing a mail box with a royal cypher said: 'I know: we shall bring him up as an Englishman.' My father, more than ever convinced of my mother's sagacity, complied.

If it should be thought that the idea of bringing up an Indo-Irishman as a Briton had something of the whimsical in it, I should say at once that in nineteen hundred and twelve it was nothing of the sort. The English were then masters of three-quarters of the earth, and in this three-quarters were both the Irish and the Indians. Had I been brought up as either of these I would have thought of the English as my equals but treated them as my masters. As an Englishman I was able to treat both the Irish and the Indians as my inferiors so long as I was careful to speak of them to their faces as my equals. This formula was the basis of an astonishing organization called the British Empire and remained so until the formula was finally understood by the subject races, when the British Empire somewhat hurriedly became the Commonwealth. Thus, even in the long view, my father's faith in my mother's sagacity was right. She brought me up as the member of a race that takes pride in itself, both for having an empire and for not having one any longer: and a pride as broadly based as that is impossible to subdue.

At school I was set to read aloud to the class the adventures of Kim, my colouring adding drama to the recital. But I preferred Tom Jones and so did my little companions to whom I would tell the story serially, after school.

During periods when other children were reading Kim, I was allowed to read more widely in the works of the master and his imitators. By this means I learned that besides the English, who were admirable, and the Indians who were also admirable but not to be relied on, there was a third sort of person. This third sort was never in the least admirable and was so persistently a traitor to all his acquaintances that it was a marvel that he could ever find anyone to trust him. This third sort of person was called a Eurasian.

School Times

I asked one of my schoolteachers what 'Eurasian' meant, but she blushed deeply and passed me on to the headmaster who said I would understand when I was older but what I must always remember that Jesus loved me.

I did not think of myself as one of these unfortunates at the time, and care was taken by my schoolteachers that I wouldn't think so in the future. Their principles were liberal and so were their fees. They did not want my father to withdraw me. They saw to it that I was not caused any embarrassment which might have hurt them more than it might hurt me. They therefore set about my education in this important matter with a will. I was rapidly made to understand that by great good fortune and a paternal Act of Parliament I had been compulsorily registered within a short time of my having seen the light as having been born in England.

So I was an Englishman! Hurray for that, said my teachers. For a shilling at Somerset House I could get a copy of my birth certificate to prove it.

But this brought responsibilities with it and looking back I can see that these responsibilities weighed more on my instructors' consciences than they did on mine. I particularly worried all my teachers, from the mistresses of my infancy to the headmaster who sent me into the wider world, in the matter of telling the truth. Not that I was mendacious; but I so easily might have been with my mixed ancestry. An Englishman's word was his bond. It was especially important that I should learn this because I might very well spend parts of my life in, say, the Orient, and it was there above all other places that the Englishman was respected as a man who told the truth. This great virtue of his did not count for so much in England. Indeed there, one Englishman often told such black lies to another Englishman that the only way of getting at the truth was British Justice. This was the best in the world. But in dealing with foreigners, especially coloured races, an Englishman should always

My Grandmother and the Dirty English

stick to the truth, although this was recognised to be no small part of the white man's burden.

Thus by virtue of my birth certificate, my boyhood was spent, not in embittered isolation, but in the kindly company of people only too anxious to make me like themselves.

My grandmother, like Michelangelo, had *terribilià*. She had a driving will; she would not be baulked and whatever she did was designed to strike the spectator with awe. She was also something of a stick. She rarely spoke to anyone who was not of her own social station and she received them formally: that is to say, with her breasts completely bare. Even with time women were growing lax about this custom in Malabar but my grandmother insisted on it. She thought that married women who wore blouses and pretty saris were jezebels; in her view, a wife who dressed herself above her waist could only be aiming at adultery.

When I was twelve, she demanded that I be brought and shown to her. I was incontinently taken half across the earth, from London to south of the town of Calicut. My mother came with me.

The last part of the journey was made by dug-out canoe (there being no railways and no good roads near our family estate) and in this we were poled on a moonlit night up the Ponani river. The river was lined with palm trees and crocodiles.

My mother taking fright at these beasts, I sang to keep them away from the boat. I sang a song I had been taught at school called 'Drake's Drum'. I had been taught many songs with similar sentiments but this was the noisiest. I sang it with a will because my young heart (especially in such very foreign parts) glowed with the sentiment.

This singing marked a stage in my life. Shortly afterwards I lost my innocence. My grandmother took me in hand and I never thought the English were perfect again.

School Times

When my grandmother had heard that my mother intended to make the visit as well as myself, she had given orders for a special house to be put in repair for my mother's accommodation. It was on the furthest confines of the family property. This was her solution to a difficult problem. My mother was ritually unclean, and therefore whenever she entered my family house, she would defile it. The house would have to be purified. It followed logically that if my mother stayed in the house, it would be permanently in a state of defilement and permanently in a state of being ritually cleaned. Since this ceremony involved drums and conch shells, my mother's visit foreshadowed a prolonged uproar. All this was avoided by my grandmother's decision to put her up in a separate building.

I cannot say that my grandmother was ever rude to my mother. She never referred to her by name but always as 'the Englishwoman'. This was not necessarily an insulting expression, but my mother had Irish blood and what with thus, and the house, and some other pinpricks, her temper rose. She ordered a quantity of medical stores from Calicut, and when they arrived she set up a free dispensary on the verandah, to which the peasants flocked. It was an admirably devised answer. My grandmother had shut the door in my mother's face. She now had the galling experience of seeing my mother industriously cleaning up the doorstep. As my mother well knew, each drop of iodine that she dispensed stung not only the grateful patient, but also my grandmother's conscience.

My grandmother brooded on this for a while and then sent my mother a bag of golden sovereigns. My mother, taking this to be a bribe at the worst, or at the best, a tip, sent it back. But she was wrong. It was a peace offering. It was sent again next day, accompanied by the family goldsmith who sat, slept and ate on the verandah for one week while he made the sovereigns (with tweezers and a charcoal fire) into a great gold collar which my mother still, on occasion, wears.

My Grandmother and the Dirty English

When, fourteen years before my trip, my father had written from England to say that he was getting married to a white woman, my grandmother had been far from giving the union her blessing. But it would be wrong to say that she had objected to it. If an English boy of twenty-two wrote home from foreign parts to say that he had taken to cannibalism, his parents would not object. They would be so revolted that a mere objection would never meet the case. So with my grandmother.

She had never met the English but she knew all about them. She knew they were tall, fair, given to strong drink, good soldiers and that they had conquered her native country. She also knew that they were incurably dirty in their personal habits. She respected them but wished they would keep their distance. It was very much the way that a Roman matron looked upon the Goths.

My eldest uncle had been to England for two years and he spoke up for the English. He said that while the Hindus were undoubtedly the most civilized race on earth and had been civilized a thousand years before the English, nevertheless, the English were now the masters of the Hindus. My grandmother's reply to this was that the English were masters of the Hindus only because 'nobody would listen to us'. By this she meant that our family, along with others of the same caste, had strongly objected to Vasco da Gama being allowed to land in Calicut. They had, in fact, done their best to get him and his sailors massacred. But the country was not behind them and he escaped. Everything, my grandmother argued (and not without some reason), had started with that.

But her chief complaint was that the English were so dirty, and this was rather a poser for my uncle. When my grandmother asked if, like decent people, they took a minimum of two baths a day, my uncle, who could not lie to his mother without committing a disgraceful sin, said that, well, no: but a few took one bath and the habit was spreading. He could go no further than that. But he added that my grandmother should remember that England had a cold climate. This she loyally did, and when she discussed the matter with me she was able to treat the matter lightly, as one does the disgusting but rational liking of the Eskimos for eating blubber.

As for the question of eating, she did not have the expected prejudices. She did not think it strange that the English ate ham and beef. The outcast hill-tribes (called Todas), who made the family straw mats and cleaned the latrines, ate anything. She was not disturbed, either, about their religion, because my uncle assured her that they had practically none. Their manners, however, she abominated. If she did not mind them eating meat, she considered their way of eating it beyond the pale of decent society. In my family home, each person eats his meal separately, preferably in a secluded corner. The thought that English people could sit opposite to each other and watch each other thrust food into their mouths, masticate, and swallow it, made her wonder if there was anything that human beings would not do, when left to their own devices.

With this background, then, my grandmother's peace offering of a bag of sovereigns was a considerable victory for my mother, particularly since the gold collar which the goldsmith had been told to make from them was the characteristic jewellery of a Malabar bride.

The way was now open for me. I could go and see her. I had waited about three weeks.

I had many meetings with her. I used to visit her inconsiderable state. The distance from our home — the isolation wing, so to speak — to the main family mansion was too far for walking in the Malabar sun. I used to go by palanquin. It was a hammock of red cloth with rather worn embroidery of gold thread, and it was swung on a black pole which had silver ornaments at either end. Four virtually naked men, two in front and two behind, carried the palanquin at a swift trot. There was considerable art in this. If the four trotted just as they

My Grandmother and the Dirty English

pleased, the hammock would swing in a growing arc until it tipped the passenger out on to the road. To prevent this, the men trotted in a complicated system that I never really understood: watching them and trying to trace it out was as difficult as trying to determine the order in which a horse puts its hoofs down. They kept their rhythm by chanting. I used to fall asleep on the way, listening to them. It must have presented an interesting spectacle — a red palanquin, the sweating men, and a sleeping schoolboy wearing an English blazer with its pocket sewn with a badge gained by infantile prowess at some sport that I do not now remember.

My grandmother usually received me sitting by her favourite box in her boudoir. She made an unforgettable picture. She had great black eyes, a shock of white hair, and lips as lush and curved as a girl of eighteen. The skin of her bosom, bare as I have said, was quite smooth. I used to sit on the floor in front of her in my school blazer and since my father had never taught me Malayalam (wishing me to be brought up like any other English schoolboy), we talked through one of my uncles.

The things my grandmother told me were a puzzle at the time. But I have come to understand them better. Much as she looked down on the English, I think that had she met some of them, had she overcome her well-bred fastidiousness and actually mixed with them, she would have found she and they had much in common. Her riding passion, like theirs, was racial pride.

She felt that she was born of a superior race and she had all the marks of it. For instance, she deplored the plumbing of every other nation but her own. She would often say to me: 'Never take a bath in one of those contraptions in which you sit in dirty water like a buffalo. Always bathe in running water. A really nice person does not even glance at his own bath water, much less sit in it.' Here she would laugh to herself, while my uncle translated; not an unkind laugh, but a pitying one, as she thought of the backwardness of the white man's bathroom.

But a grandson was a grandson, even though her permission had not been sought to bring him into the world, and she set about being a mother as well as a grandmother to me. She knew that soon I would go back among the heathen to finish my education, and she wanted me to go back knowing who and what I was. On one of my visits she gave me a small book in which was written all my duties and privileges as a member of my class. The book was written on dried palm leaves, strung together with a cord between two covers of wood. It began with a prayer to God thanking Him for creating us — our caste, that is — so much superior in every respect to the great majority of other human beings.

My grandmother explained what followed several times and with much emphasis, for she wanted to imprint it on my memory. Our family belongs to the caste or class — called Nayars. The Nayars of Malabar are as old as Indian history and therefore, it can be assumed, a good deal older. My grandmother told me that traditionally we had two obligations to society. We were warriors when there was battle, and when there was not, we had the duty, on certain holy days, of carrying flowers to the temple.

I remember that I thought this very romantic at the time and could not understand why my grandmother took it so prosaically: to me, warriors, flowers and temples conjured up a picture of some Oriental Round Table. But my grandmother was right. Our caste is a common place; it exists everywhere. In England it is scattered all over the countryside. The men are what is called 'Army' and the women take not only flowers, but fruit to the temple on the occasion of the harvest festival. It is curious and inexplicable, that the combination of these two activities whether in the Shires or in the coconut groves of Malabar, produces the most ferocious snobs.

But my grandmother was quite ignorant of these striking

My Grandmother and the Dirty English

resemblances and begged me when moving among the English to remember myself. 'They will look up to you, as a Nayar, to set an example,' she used to say. 'They know that you have two thousand years of advantage over them and they will be willing to learn. Show them this book. They will be very interested. It was written when they still went about naked. And I will give you some trinkets which you can hand out as gifts: some amulets which we use and some things made of sandalwood, which is very rare in England, so I am told, and much sought after. They will help you make friends. But remember, it is your example which will count more than anything.'

She gave me all the things she promised and as she had foretold, they were much admired. Some of them, I believe, are still in my school museum. She also gave me her blessing, which was what I had been brought across the world to get.

I thought over her advice but I was in some confusion. My headmaster, wishing me goodbye and good luck when I had set out on my trip, had said much the same thing. 'Let them see,' he had said, 'by your example that you have been trained in an English school. Wherever you go, it is for you to set the tone.' He did not give me any sandalwood, but I was very impressed. I was also very impressed with what my grandmother had said.

— From *Dead Man in the Silver Market*
(First published in *The New Yorker* of 4 July 1953)

Prep School

Lord Berners

WE WERE GREETED BY MRS Gambril, the headmaster's wife. Her round face with its rather bare expression and her sleek auburn hair dragged off the forehead reminded me forcibly of a horse-chestnut. She was dressed very fashionably yet she had the unmistakable air of an 'official' woman, as it might be female warder or the superintendent of a workhouse. She had a sister, Miss Temple, who helped her to run the non-didactic departments of the, school. Miss Temple was a replica of her sister, but with the subtle distinction of spinsterhood; she was slightly more angular and less suave.

Mr Gambril joined us at luncheon. His appearance was surprising. I had never in my life seen anyone quite so yellow. His skin was yellow, his hair was yellow and he had a small yellow moustache carefully waxed at the ends. I discovered later that he smoked cigarettes incessantly ... He certainly looked as though tobacco juice flowed in his veins, and whenever he grew angry there would be an additional rush of it to his face, which became a deep mahogany. He had very small light blue eyes that appeared all the more striking for being set in their complementary colour. He wore a grey frock-coat and one of those flat, elaborate satin ties folded like a table-napkin and fastened with a large diamond scarf-pin.

At luncheon that day nobody could have been more urbane. He was exercising the charm specially reserved for parents. He patted me on the head, smiled at me and said, 'We shall make a man of him.'

Prep School

So far it had not been very alarming; a polite and amiable host, two benevolent middle-aged ladies and a pleasant dining-room looking out on to a garden. One might have been visiting neighbours. I felt slightly reassured, and thought that I might perhaps be going to enjoy being at school.

This emotional respite lasted until my mother's departure. Then, as the train steamed out of the station, I was suddenly overcome by the sensation that it was bearing away from me not only my mother but the whole of that home life to which, in spite of a certain ennui and restlessness, I had become fondly attached, leaving me alone in a new and unsympathetic world.

Mr Gambril had accompanied us to the station. On the way back 1 noticed a distinct change in his manner. He was no longer the amiable friend of the family An official chasm had opened between us. He seemed all of a sudden to have grown immensely large and I infinitesimally small. The personal note had vanished. He now spoke to me in a voice that might have been directed at any small boy.

On returning to the house he took me to his study, that grim chamber, the scene of many a future agony. My mind, from the stress of emotion, had become a hyper-sensitive retina upon which every detail stood out with an almost painful distinctness. The rows of solemn-looking dictionaries and primers on the bookshelves, the bust of an elderly gentleman of forbidding aspect on the mantelpiece (Mr Gambril Senior, the former headmaster), and in a corner, near the window, an ominous group of canes and birches.

Mr Gambril selected a number of books from the shelves and handed them to me. 'These are the books you will require. Put them in your locker and don't lose them! You will be shown where your locker is. Lucy dear!' he called — Mrs Gambril appeared — 'take this boy and show him his locker.'

Mrs Gambril led me through a green baize door that separated the headmaster's quarters from the rest of the school. She showed me the different classrooms, the huge Assembly Room that could accommodate the entire school (there were over a hundred boys in all) and the Lobby, a wide and rather dark passage running down the middle of the building and leading into the Assembly Room on one side and into the smaller classrooms on the other. At the end of the Lobby there was a large glass door opening on to the playground. My newly acquired school books were deposited in my locker, including my other belongings and the beloved four volumes of *British Birds* with coloured illustrations, which my mother, rather reluctantly, had allowed me to take with me.

The barren appearance of the classrooms and the general aspect of the school furniture struck a chill into my heart. I felt as strange, as forlorn as if I had been visiting the mountains of the moon. Everything looked so uncomfortable, so hard and utilitarian, and the air was heavy with the cheerless smell of fresh paint and furniture polish.

In the playground outside I caught sight of two disconsolate figures. 'Those,' said Mrs Gambril, 'are the two other new boys, Arthur and Creeling.'

The name Arthur revived memories of Tom Brown. But at that moment I was very far from wishing to have to champion anyone. A 'little Arthur' would have only been an additional embarrassment.

Mrs Gambril left me in their company. Arthur was not in the least like his namesake. To begin with, he was one of the ugliest little boys I had ever seen. His face looked as though it belonged to the vegetable rather than to the human anatomy. His features gave one the impression of being bruised and swollen, and his eyes were red with weeping. Creeling was better-looking, but he had a sanctimonious expression that repelled me. He looked like a miniature curate.

Upon seeing me they both made a visible effort to pull themselves together and to appear a little less despondent, but it was not very successful. I, myself, was hovering on the brink of tears.

Creeling, who was a little older than Arthur and myself, tried to assume a moral leadership. 'You must never,' he advised us, 'let other fellows find out the Christian names of your sisters.'

'I haven't any sisters,' I replied with some asperity. In spite of my woefully flagging spirits I resented his attitude of Mentor.

As Arthur appeared to be practically speechless, the conversation, such as it was, was carried on between Creeling and myself. Timidly and as though we felt we were trespassing, we visited the playing fields, the cricket pavilion, the fives courts, the lavatories, the swimming bath, and Creeling made an unsuccessful attempt to get into the chapel.

'They have a service every day' he remarked, 'and on Sundays three times.'

The prospect seemed to cheer him, but Arthur gulped and said, 'How awful!' in a horror-stricken voice, and his face grew more swollen and bruised in appearance than ever.

After a time the other boys began to arrive. Creeling, Arthur and I clung together disconsolately in a corner of the Lobby. I prayed that we might remain unobserved for as long as possible. Hitherto, the presence of my contemporaries at children's parties or at the dancing class had never inspired me with the slightest feeling of shyness; the background of home life had given me a certain sense of security and on such occasions there had always been a mother, a nurse or a governess in the offing. Now, however, I was bereft of these aids to confidence, and I knew that I would have to fend for myself.

It was not long before we were noticed. A group of boys from the far end of the Lobby bore down upon us with whoops and cries of 'New boys!' It was an awful moment; a moment of suspense such as explorers must go through on the appearance of an unknown savage tribe.

These cannibals, however, proved comparatively friendly. It is true there were one or two youths whose practice it was to kick new boys, but it was done with an absence of malice that made me realize that it was a formality rather than an act of hostility. The ordeal of being asked one's name was not so terrible after all, and I began to gather confidence.

I created a favourable impression by exhibiting my books of *British Birds*. Next to being good at games a taste for natural history was highest in popular esteem; but I was not aware of this at the time, and I fear it was merely one of those impulses which sometimes tempt us to try and enhance our personality by reverting to our possessions. Anyhow the move was a successful one, and the mild popularity I acquired by offering to lend some of the volumes helped to carry me through supper, which would otherwise have depressed me with its long refectory tables covered with coarse linen, the plates and tea-cups of monumental solidity, the chunks of bread-and-butter and slices of stringy cold meat of a similar calibre and the over-sweetened tepid tea poured out of metal jugs, gulped down to the accompaniment of a deafening roar of conversation.

As soon as supper was over, a bell rang and we all trooped into the chapel. Mr Gambril made his appearance clad in a surplice. He was followed by the assistant masters. After a short address on the subject of the reassembling of school, to which I listened in a spirit of reverent attention, there followed prayers and a hymn. The lamplight, the music and that odd musty smell peculiar to English Protestant churches combined to work upon my feelings. My eyes filled with tears and everything became a blur.

In my dormitory there were seven or eight small boys of about the same age as myself. Apart from Creeling, Arthur and myself they were all second term boys and they all seemed to be suffering from home sickness. From the other dormitories, there came shouts of hilarity, but in ours depression reigned. After we had undressed

Prep School

and stowed away our clothes in wicker baskets under our beds, a manservant walked through the rooms ringing a bell, the signal for private devotions. Each boy knelt down by his bedside. (There was not going to be any 'little Arthur' nonsense about prayers). Soon afterwards Mr Gambril appeared, followed by the Matron, and said good night to each of us in turn. This was a special act of kindness to new boys on the first evening and the ceremony was not repeated on subsequent nights. Finally, one of the assistant masters came in and turned out the gas.

Misery descended upon me with the darkness. For a long time I lay awake. So apparently did most of the other occupants of the dormitory, for the air was full of the sound of muffled sobbing.

Through a chink in the blinds I could see: that there was bright moonlight outside, and through the half-open window I could hear the nocturnal sounds of the country, the lowing of cattle in a neighbouring field, the cry of a night-bird, the whistle of a distant train (wending its way northwards perhaps, in the direction of Althrey), and from the garden below there came up a faint scent of lilac. Now that the turmoil of human contact had died away, all these things reminded me poignantly of my far-off home. My mother, the servants, the garden with its flowers and its birds, appeared to me like the sad ghosts of a past that was now gone forever. I even thought regretfully of Mademoiselle Bock.

I remembered the four volumes of *British Birds* in my locker. These seemed now to constitute the only link with home life.

— From *First Childhood*

A Pair of Steel Spectacles

Richard Church

I THINK IT IS THE gnostics who belive that the soul is born when we are seven years old. I am inclined, from my own experience, to believe this dogma, and I base my belief on the events of that wonderful year, the first of the new century.

It began with the setting up of the aquarium in the bay window of the kitchen, overlooking the long and only flowerbed in the yard. The afternoon sun struck the back of the house, and threw a thwart beam across that window, penetrating into the aquarium and lighting up its occupants, so that they shone like lighted ships.

I cannot count what hours I wasted, if they were wasted, gazing into that distant world. When the slant sun of summer evenings struck the aquarium, the effect was so overwhelming that 1 stood there almost in tears. Sometimes at night, when the gaslight threw a sombre beam into the tank, I was equally moved, but with more tragic and foreboding an emphasis, for in this refraction the weeds had become dark emblems of despair, and the golden creatures subdued to a sluggish resignation, their tarnished sides immobile, except for a petulant movement of cavernous mouths and the supporting rhythm of the transparent fore-fins, no longer luminous.

It may be that the other-world scenery within the glass walls of Jack's aquarium so played upon my imagination that my sluggish wits were at last awakened. I knew that about that time, the end-of-winter weeks before my seventh birthday in March, the

A Pair of Steel Spectacles

concentration with which I stared into that small tank (much to the amusement of the family) began to be applied to the rest of the world around me. I saw things with much more particularity, and I was aware also of my curious pleasure in this recognition of detail.

No doubt the improvement was optical as much as mental. A medical examination at school had revealed the fact that I was shortsighted. The doctor took me solemnly between his knees, looked into my face, and said, 'If you don't get some glasses, you'll be blind by the time you are fifteen, and I shall tell your parents so.'

I was rather proud of this distinction. Fifteen! That was so far ahead that it meant nothing to me, except a sort of twilight at the end of life. My parents thought otherwise, and one Saturday afternoon I was taken, via a steep road called Pig Hill, to a chemist's shop on Lavender Hill, Glapham, opposite the first theatre that I was ever to enter, 'The Shakespeare'. Behind the shop was a room where my eyes were tested in the rough and ready way customary in those days. The chemist hung an open framework that felt like the Forth Bridge around my ears and on my nose. Lenses were slotted into this, and twisted about, while I was instructed to read the card of letters beginning with a large 'E'.

I still remember the astonishment with which I saw the smaller letters change from a dark blur into separate items of the alphabet. I thought about it all the following week, and found that by screwing up my eyes when I was out of doors I could get to some faint approximation of that clarity, for a few seconds at a time.

This made me surmise that the universe which, hitherto, I had seen as a vague mass of colour and blurred shapes might in actuality be much more concise and defined. I was, therefore, half-prepared for the surprise which shook me a week later when, on the Saturday evening, we went again to the shop on Lavender Hill, and the chemist produced the bespoken pair of steel-rimmed spectacles through which I was invited to read the card. I read it, from top to bottom! I turned, and looked in triumph at mother, but what I saw was mother intensified. I saw the pupils of her eyes, the tiny feathers in her boa necklet; I saw the hairs in father's moustache, and on the back of his hand. Jack's cap might have been made of metal, so hard and clear did it shine on his close-cropped head, above his bony face and huge nose. I saw his eyes too, round, inquiring, fierce with a hunger of observation. He was studying me with a gimlet sharpness such as I had never before been able to perceive.

Then we walked out of the shop, and I stepped on to the pavement, which came up and hit me, so that I had to grasp the nearest support — father's coat. 'Take care, now, take care!' he said indulgently (though he disapproved of all these concessions to physical weakness). 'And mind you don't break them!'

I walked still with some uncertainty, carefully placing my feet and feeling their impact on the pavement whose surface I could see sparkling like quartz in the lamplight.

The lamplight! I looked in wonder at the diminishing crystals of gas-flame strung down the hill. Clapham was hung with necklaces of light, and the horses pulling the glittering omnibuses struck the granite road with hooves of iron and ebony. I could see the skeletons inside the flesh and blood of the Saturday-night shoppers. The garments they wore were made of separate threads. In this new world, sound as well as sight was changed. It took on hardness and definition, forcing itself upon my hearing, so that I was besieged simultaneously through the eye and through the ear.

How willingly I surrendered! I went out to meet this blazing and trumpeting invasion. I trembled with the excitement, and had to cling to mother's arm to prevent myself being carried away in the flood as the pavements rushed at me, and people loomed up with their teeth like tusks, their lips luscious, their eyes bolting out of their heads, bearing down on me as they threw out spears of conversation that whizzed loudly past my ears and bewildered my wits.

A Pair of Steel Spectacles

'Is it any different?' asked Jack, in his proprietary voice. He was never satisfied until he had collected all possible information on everything which life brought to his notice.

'It makes things clearer,' I replied, knowing that I had no hope of telling him what was happening to me. I was only half-aware of it myself, for this urgent demand upon my attention made by the multitudinous world around me was the beginning of a joyous imposition to which I am still responding today, breathless and enraptured, though the twilight of the senses begins to settle.

My excitement must have communicated itself to the rest of the family, for father proposed that, instead of our going home to supper, we should have the meal at The Creighton, an Italian restaurant near Clapham Junction. This was the first time in my life that I ate in public, and I remember it so clearly because the tablecloth appeared to be made of white ropes in warp and woof, and the cutlery had an additional hardness, beyond that of ordinary steel and plate. When the food came to the table, the steam rising from it was as coarse as linen. I saw the spots of grease on the waiter's apron, and the dirt under his fingernails.

All this emphasis made me shy, as I would have been, indeed, without this optical exaggeration that had the effect of thrusting me forward, to be seen as conspicuously as I now saw everything and everybody around me. But I ate my fried plaice, dissecting it with a new skill, since every bone was needle-clear. Our parents drank stout, their usual supper glass. Jack and I had ginger-beer, a rare luxury that added to the formality of the feast.

By the time we reached the darker streets near home, my head ached under the burden of too much seeing. Perhaps the grease of the fried fish, and the lateness of the hour, had something to do with the exhaustion that almost destroyed me as we trailed homeward. The new spectacles clung to my face, eating into the bridge of my nose and behind the earlobes. I longed to tear them off and throw

School Times

them away into the darkness. I tried to linger behind, so that at least I might secrete them in the pocket of my blouse.

But before I could further this purpose, something caught my attention. I realised that, after all, the side-streets were not quite dark; that the yellow pools around each gas-lamp, now as clearly defined as golden sovereigns, were augmented, pervaded, suffused by a bluish silver glory. I looked upward, and saw the sky. And in that sky I saw an almost full moon, floating in space, a solid ball of roughened metal, with an irregular jagged edge. I could put up my hand and take it, ponder its weight, feel its cold surface.

I stopped walking, and stared. I turned up my face, throwing back my head to look vertically into the zenith. I saw the stars, and I saw them for the first time, a few only, for most were obscured by the light of the moon; but those I saw were clean pin-points of light, diamond-hard, standing not upon a velvet surface, but floating in space, some near, some far, in an awe-striking perspective that came as a revelation to my newly educated eyes. I felt myself swept up into that traffic of the night sky. I floated away, and might have disappeared into space had not a cry recalled me.

It was mother's voice,, in alarm, for she had looked round, perhaps impatiently, to urge me along, only to see me lying on my back on the pavement, in a state of semi-coma. Father picked me up, and I was still too far gone to resent being carried like a baby I knew, however, that Jack would have something to say when we got to bed, for he would accuse me of showing off, or creating a scene. He had a horror of any form of demonstration, and he discouraged extravagance and self-indulgence, two weaknesses which he was always prepared to detect in me, and to correct.

— From *Over the Bridge*

The Phantom Ship Steered by a Dead Man's Hand

Matthew Henry Barker

The Phantom Ship is no mere fiction of authors who write about the sea. In the days of sailing ships, there was, among the sailors, a widespread belief in such ghostly craft, and an equally wide diversity of lower-deck opinion as to what their appearance portended. And if there was ever a sailor who could tell all the tales of them, that man was Matthew Henry Barker. For in the early days of the nineteenth century, Barker, when hardly more than a boy, joined an East Indiaman, and afterwards the Royal Navy - in which, as he was without influence, he never rose beyond master's mate. Then, about 1824, he retired from the sea, and took to yarning on paper, producing — always under the name of "The Old Sailor" — a number of spirited sea tales, which were very popular in their days.

TOWARDS NIGHT, THE WARLOCK'S COURSE was changed to a more northerly direction, and every eye was wakeful, in the hope of winning so rich a prize. Often were the glasses put in requisition, and eager hope ran high — to meet with disappointment; repeatedly did the seamen point out some fancied object to each other, which they insisted was the schooner's white sails, but which only existed in their own imaginations, or was the silvery foam of some curling billow. The corvette was travelling at a famous rate, brightening still more her already shining coppers as she rushed through the yielding element, and manifesting the power of the winds against the resistance of the waters. It was just the breeze that sailors love, and 'The Wizard of the Sea,' like a sportive seagull, seemed to exult in her speed. Merrily she flew, boldly dashing through the crest of each rolling wave, and scattering away the spray in many thousand particles from her finely-moulded bows.

'A starn chase is a long chase,' exclaimed one of the seamen amongst a group of his shipmates in the same watch, collected together in the lee waste, 'but if that same yampy-yam consarn of a craft doesn't sail like a witch, we ought to be nearing her fast,—' cause way, my hearties? D'ye mind, she has had but light winds to seaward, whilst we have brought the breeze along with us; and, in consequence, must have been coming up with her hand-over-hand.

'We can't have run past her,' said a second, in a tone of voice that expressed more of doubt than certainty 'I'm sartin there's been a good look-out kept by both officers and men.'

'There's no telling, Joe,' said a third, hitching up his trousers, and looking round at his watch-mates, as if to collect their opinions. After all, I'm rather misdoubtful as to the cha-rackter of that same schooner - I means as to her 'dentity among craft as has been properly baptised with a Christian name,' and he shook his head.

'It stands to reason, shipmate,' said the other, in a more determinate manner. 'Not but I'm thinking yon craft's like a flying fish, that knows the dolphin's after her; if she can't get through the water quick enough, why she'll make a spring over all, and only come down to dip nows and thens. She's too beautiful to be the work of mortal hands, and I see, shipmates, you begins to think wi' me, that there was plenty of fire to heat the pitch that pay'd her seams.'

'As for the matter o' that, if you go to look for beauty in a craft,' responded one of the carpenter's mates, who had been an old shipwright, 'then look at the handsome model under your feet. Why, there's not a sweeter piece o' framework in the world: she's as lively as a cricket, and as fleet as a hound.'

'True, Bill, true,' returned Joe, laying his hand upon his

messmate's shoulder, and approaching his mouth towards his ear as he added, in a cautious half-whisper, 'but is there no devilry about her? Do you think she was modelled only by human judgment?'

The carpenter's mate was silent, for he knew there was a rumour in the ship that the man who built the Warlock was supposed to have dealings with the great tempter of mankind, and he had destroyed himself on hearing of her capture. The mysteriousness of their captain was also presented to his mind, and a strong feeling of superstition seemed to be fast overpowering the whole group, and they remained without speaking for several minutes.

'Keep a good look-out before, there,' shouted the officer of the watch, and his voice came with a startling vehemence upon the stillness of the night. The 'ay ay, sir,' was immediately responded, and the seamen again fell into conversation. 'Well, shipmates,' said Joe, 'you may say and think as you will; but I'm blow'd if I don't believe that same schooner is but a phantom-craft, as the devil keeps for a pleasure-boat. There's many on 'em here and there scudding about upon the ocean; and the skippers when they're hard up in a clinch, and want to escape overhauling, have only to hail their owner for a fog-bank, which they creep into and disappear, just as a sarpent would riggle itself into a field o' guinea-grass. But, mark my word, Jem, if we don't see summut afore long as will throw us all slap aback with wonderment. I never liked the look o' that 'ere Spanish chap as was aboard the other night at the sheave-o. I kept my eyes fixed on his starn, expecting every moment to twig his outrigger, but I s'pose he had coiled it away in a Flemish fake abaft; and he took precious good care not to unship his hat, lest we should diskiver his head-rails. Ay? Ay; I don't care what others may know o' the matter; I'm—if it warn't Davy Jones himself, it wur one of his near relations.'

Avast! Joe avast!' said another, who had not spoken before, but had listened with devoted attention. 'You know we all thought that Jack Spaniard was another guess sort of a person — one who—' and he canted his hand over his shoulder towards the captain's cabin. 'And as for ould Devy,' he continued, 'I'm thinking the skipper wouldn't care the fag-end of a tinker's — for him, if so be he could clap him fairly alongside. But as to this here schooner as we're chasing, why mayhap she's within hail now, only she's invisible.'

'Mayhap so! mayhap so!' returned the individual addressed, 'for there's no telling what a cloud may conceal. I remembers once being off the Cape in a fresh o' wind, for the devil had spread his dirty cloth over the Table Land, and so the hands were turned up, reef topsels. I warn't in a man-o'-war then, shipmates — I was in an Ingeeman, bound to Madras and Bengal. Well, as I was a saying, the hands were turned up, reef topsels; it was the middle watch, somewhere about five bells, and it looked squally and sneezing away to the nor'-west, with the scud flying over our heads like a shoal of black spirits riding on the wind, and chasing each other for sport. Well, shipmates, I was then only a youngster, doing duty in the mizzen-top; and so I got the clew-lines stretched along, and the topsel-sheets all clear for letting go, and then I waits for the other watch to come up afore we went aloft. All at once I seed a large ship away upon the weather-beam, coming down upon us under every stitch of canvas as a craft can set, — studd'n-sels a both sides, alow and aloft, though it was blowing very hard at the time; and we'd as much as we could hang on, with double-reefed topsels and the top-gall'nt masts struck. So when I seed her, I sings out, "Sail, O!" though, shipmates, I'll swear, point blank, she warn't in sight two minutes afore. So, as I was a saying, I sings, out, "Sail, O, to windward! Port your helm!"— for the larboard side was the weather-side; — "port your helm! port! or she'll be aboard of us!" Well, the captain jumps up upon the poop, alongside o' me, and he seed the craft, and he halloos through his speaking-trumpet to the man at the weather-wheel, "Port, lad! Hard up with the helm! Square away the after-yards!" But before she could be got to answer her helm, I'm blest if the stranger's flying-jib-boom wasn't right over us, just abaft the mizen-rigging; and so, expecting that we should get our quarters stove in, and mayhap obligated to swim for it, I claps my arms round a loose hen-coop, by way of a Noah's ark, and houlds on like grim death agen the doctor. So I waits and waits for the crash; but, to my wonderment, I didn't never feel not nothing whatsoever touch us. There was no shock, no noise, and so I looked up to windward, and I couldn't get the smallest blink of her; but when I looked to board, there she was, close to us on our lee-quarter, going steadily afore it, without a yard of a quarter-point either way, and carrying on as taut a press as ever. We never seed a single creetur aboard of her, nor heard the creaking of a spar, nor the rattle of a block. She had a high Dutch starn, and steady she went, rolling along like the white-shrouded ghost of a giant, seemingly without straining a rope-yarn. And well she might go steady, shipmates,' added the seaman, in a voice of solemnitye, — 'well she might go steady, seeing she was steered by a dead man's hand.' Here he paused for a minute or two, and then resumed. 'Well! What was the upshot of it? Why, shipmates, if it didn't come on to blow great guns directly afterwards, then I never seed it blow great guns in my life. In less than an hour, we were hove-to under a close-reefed main-topsel, in a sea running as high as a church steeple. One o' the fleet was missing next morning, and was never heard on afterwards.'

— Matthew Henry Barker: *The Warlock (1860)*

What Happened to a Father Who Became a Schoolboy

F. Anstey

Perhaps it would be a good thing if some fathers were transformed into boys and went to school again. But perhaps it would not be so good if boys were suddenly changed into heavy-weight seniors. What might happen in both cases was the original idea of an amusing book, 'Vice Versa,' or 'A Lesson to Fathers', by Thomas Anstey Guthrie. The father in 'Vice Versa,' Mr Paul Multitude, was bidding goodbye in a sermonizing way to his son Dick, who was not very keen — at any rate, for the moment — about returning to school. Dick handed his father a curious stone which his Uncle Duke had brought from India, and which had magic powers of fulfilling the first wish expressed by whoever held the stone. Mr Bultitude, as fathers will do, happened to say that he wished he could be like Dick again — and lo! He became a boy. Feeling himself to be in a ridiculous position, he tried to wish himself back to his former self; but the Garuda stone did not work that way. He gave the stone to Dick, thinking that he might wish things back as they were. But Dick, realizing his unique opportunity to escape school, uttered his own wish — and lo! He became Bultitude senior.

'WHAT DID YOU SAY?' GASPED PAUL.

'Why, you see,' exclaimed Dick, 'it would never have done for us both to go back; the chaps would have humbugged us so; and as I hate the place, and you seem so fond of being a boy and going back to school and that, I thought perhaps it would be best for you to go

What Happened to a Father Who Became a Schoolboy

and see how you liked it!'

'I never will! I'll not stir from this room! I dare you to try to move me!' cried Paul. And just then there was the sound of wheels outside once more. They stopped before the house, the bell rang sharply — the long-expected cab had come at last.

'You've no time to lose,' said Dick, 'get your coat on.'

Mr Bultitude tried to treat the affair as a joke. He laughed a ghastly little laugh.

'Ha! ha! You've fairly caught your poor old father this time; you've proved him wrong. I admit I said more than I exactly meant. But that's enough. Don't drive a good joke too far; shake hands, and let us see if we can't find a way out of this!'

But Dick only warmed his coat tails at the fire as he said, with a very ungenerous reminiscence of his father's manner: 'You are going back to an excellent establishment, where you will enjoy all the comforts of home — I can particularly recommend the stick jaw; look out for it on Tuesdays and Fridays. You will once more take part in the games and lessons of happy boyhood. (Did you ever play 'chevy' before when you were a boy? You'll enjoy 'chevy'.) And you will find your companions easy enough to get on with, if you don't go giving yourself airs; they won't stand airs. Now goodbye, my boy, and bless you!'

Paul stood staring stupidly at this outrageous assumption; he could scarcely believe even yet that it was meant in cruel earnest. Before he could answer, the door opened and Boaler appeared.

'Had a deal of trouble to find a keb, sir, on a night like this,' he said to the false Dick, 'but the luggage is all on top, and the man says there's plenty of time still.'

'Goodbye then, my boy,' said Dick, with well-assumed tenderness, but a rather dangerous light in his eye. 'Remember, I expect you to work . . .'

School Times

[Mr Paul Bultitude, now transformed into his son, found himself being driven to the station, en route for school. In his unaccustomed surroundings there, he had a bad time — very different from that spent by Dick, according to this letter from Miss Bultitude sent to her supposed brother at the school:]

'My dearest darling Dick, I hope you have not been expecting a letter from me before this, but I had such lots to tell you that I waited till I had time to tell it all at once. For I have such news for you! You can't think how pleased you will be when you hear it. Where shall I begin? I hardly know, for it still seems so funny and strange — almost like a dream — only I hope we shall never wake up.

'I think I must tell you anyhow, just as it comes. Well, ever since you went away (how was it you never came up to say Goodbye to us in the drawing-room? We couldn't believe till we heard the door shut that you really had driven away without another word!) Where am I? Oh, ever since you went away, dear papa has been completely changed; you would hardly believe it unless you saw him. He is quite jolly and boyish — only fancy, and we are always telling him he is the biggest baby of us all, but it only makes him laugh. Once, you know, he would have been awfully angry if we had even hinted at it.

'Do you know, I really think that the real reason he was so crabby and sharp with us that last week was because you were going away; for now the wrench of parting is over, he is quite light-hearted again. You know how he always hates showing his feelings.

'He is so altered now, you can't think. He has actually only once been up to the city since you left, and then he came home at four o'clock, and he seems quite like to have us all about him. Generally, he stays at home all the morning and plays at soldiers with baby in the dining room. You would laugh to see him loading the cannons with real powder and shot, and he didn't care a bit when some of it made holes in the sideboard and smashed the looking-glass.

'We had such fun the other afternoon; we played at brigands

—papa and all of us. Papa had the upper conservatory for a robber-cave, and stood there keeping guard with your pop gun; and he wouldn't let the servants go by without a kiss, unless they showed a written pass from us! Miss McFadden called in the middle of it, but she said she wouldn't come in, as papa seemed to be enjoying himself so. Boaler has given warning, but we can't think why. We have been out nearly every evening — once to Hengler's and once to the Christy Minstrels, and last night to the Pantomime, where papa was so pleased with the clown that he sent round afterwards and asked him to dine here on Sunday, when Sir Benjamin and Lady Bangle and Alderman Fish wick are coming. Won't it be jolly to see a clown so close? Should you think he'd come in his evening dress? Miss Mangnall has been given a month's holiday, because papa didn't like to see us always at lessons. Think of that!

'We are going to have the whole house done up and refurnished at last. Papa chose the furniture for the drawing-room yesterday. It is all in yellow satin, which is rather bright, I think. I haven't seen the carpet yet, but it is to match the furniture; and there is a lovely hearthrug, with a lion-hunt worked on it.

'But that isn't the best of it; we are going to have the big children's party after all! No one but children invited, and everyone to do exactly what they like. I wanted so much to have you home for it, but papa says it would only unsettle you and take you away from your work.

'Had Dulcie forgotten you? I should like to see her so much. Now I really must leave off, as I am going to the Aquarium with papa. Mind you write me as good a letter as this is, if that old Doctor lets you. Minnie and Roly send love and kisses, and papa sends his kind regards, and I am to say he hopes you are settling down steadily to work.'

'With best love, your affectionate sister,'

'Barbara Bultitude.'

School Times

[Dulcie, mentioned in the letter, was the headmaster's daughter—between whom and Dick there had been a friendship, which Paul Bultitude of course could not continue. His troubles are complicated by a mischievous girl, who in church passes him a note, believing him to be the Dick of previous terms. The affair is discovered by the headmaster, who is about to punish the embarrassed Paul — when Dick, as Bultitude senior, visits the school:]

And still the Doctor lingered. Some kindly suggested that he was 'waxing the cane.' But the more general opinion was that he had been detained by some visitor; for it appeared that (though Paul had not noticed it) several had heard a ring at the bell. The suspense was growing more and more unbearable.

At last the door opened in a slow ominous manner, and the Doctor appeared. There was a visible change in his manner, however. The white heat of his indignation had died out: his expression was grave but distinctly softened - and he had nothing in his hand.

'I want you outside, Bultitude,' he said; and Paul, still uncertain whether, the scene of his disgrace was only about to be shifted, or what else this might mean, followed him into the hall.

'If anything can strike shame and confusion into your soul, Richard,' said the Doctor, when they were outside, 'it will be what I have to tell you now. Your unhappy father is here, in the dining room.'

Paul staggered. Had Dick, the brazen effrontery, to come here to taunt him in his slavery? What was the meaning of it? What should he say to him? He could not answer the Doctor but by a vacant stare.

'I have not seen him yet,' said the Doctor. 'He has come at a most inopportune moment (here Mr Bultitude could not agree with him). I shall allow you to meet him first, and give you the opportunity of breaking your conduct to him. I know how it will wring his paternal heart,' and the Doctor shook his head sadly and turned away.

With a curious mixture of shame, anger and impatience, Paul

What Happened to a Father Who Became a Schoolboy

turned the handle of the dining-room door. He was to meet Dick face to face once more. The final duel must be fought out between them here. Who would be the victor?

It was a strange sensation on entering to see the image of what he had so lately been standing by the mantelpiece. It gave a shock to his sense of his own identity. It seemed so impossible that that stout substantial frame could really contain Dick. For an instant, he was totally at a loss for words, and stood pale and speechless in the presence of his unprincipled son.

Dick, on his side, seemed at least as much embarrassed. He giggled uneasily, and made a sheepish offer to shake hands, which was indignantly declined.

As Paul looked he saw distinctly that his son's fraudulent imitation of his father's personal appearance had become deteriorated in many respects since that unhappy night when he had last seen it. It was then a copy, faultlessly accurate in every detail. It was now almost a caricature, a libel!

The complexion was nearly sallow, with the exception of the nose, which had rather deepened in colour. The skin was loose and flabby, and the eyes dull and a little bloodshot. But, perhaps, the greatest alteration was in the dress. Dick wore an old light tweed shooting-coat of his, and a pair of loose trousers of blue serge; while, instead of the formally tied black neckcloth his father had worn for a quarter of a century, he had a large scarf round his neck of some crude and gaudy colour; and the conventional chimney-pot hat had been discarded for a shabby old wide-brimmed felt wide-awake.

Altogether, it was by no means the costume which a British merchant, with any self-respect whatever, would select, even for a country visit.

And thus they met, as perhaps never, since this world was first set spinning down the ringing grooves of change, met father and son before!

Paul was the first to break a very awkward silence. 'You young scoundrel!' he said, with suppressed rage. 'What the devil do you mean by laughing like that? It's no laughing matter, let me tell you, sir, for one of us!'

'I can't help laughing,' said Dick, 'you do look so queer!'

'Queer! I may well look queer. I tell you that I have never, never in my whole life, spent such a perfectly infernal week as this last!'

'Ah!' observed Dick, 'I thought you wouldn't find it all jam! And yet you seemed to be enjoying yourself, too,' he said with a grin, 'from that letter you wrote.'

'What made you come here? Couldn't you be content with your miserable victory, without coming down to crow and jeer at me?'

'It is not that,' said Dick. 'I — I thought I should like to see the fellows, and find out how you were getting on, you know.' These, however, were not his only and principal motives. He had come down to get a sight of Dulcie.

'Well, sir,' said Mr Bultitude, with ponderous sarcasm, 'you'll be delighted to hear that I'm getting on uncommonly well — oh, uncommonly! Your high-spirited young friends batter me to sleep with slippers on most nights, and, as a general thing, kick me about during the day like a confounded football! And last night, sir, I was going to be expelled; and this morning I'm forgiven, and sentenced to be soundly flogged before the whole school! It was just about to take place as you came in; and I've every reason to believe it is merely postponed!'

'I say, though,' said Dick, 'you must have been going it rather, you know. I've never been expelled. Has Chawner been sneaking again? What have you been up to?'

'Nothing I solemnly swear — nothing! They're finding out things you've done, and thrashing me.'

'Well,' said Dick soothingly, 'you'll work them all off during the term, I daresay. There aren't many really bad ones. I suppose he's

What Happened to a Father Who Became a Schoolboy

seen my name cut on his writing table?'

'No, not that I'm aware of,' said Paul.

'Oh, he'd let you hear of it if he had!' said Dick. 'It's good for a whacking, that is. But, after all, what's a whacking? I never cared for a whacking.'

'But I do care, sir. I care very much, and, I tell you, I won't stand it. I can't! Dick,' he said abruptly, as a sudden hope seized him. 'You, you haven't come down here to say you're tired of your folly have you? Do you want to give it up?'

'Rather not,' said Dick. 'Why should I? No school, no lessons, nothing to do but amuse myself, eat and drink what I like, and lots of money. It's not likely, you know.'

'Have you ever thought that you're bringing yourself within reach of the law, sir?' said Paul, trying to frighten him. 'Perhaps you don't know that there's an offence known as "false personation with intent to defraud," and that it's a felony. That's what you're doing at this moment, sir!'

'Not any more than you are!' retorted Dick. 'I never began it. I had as much right to wish to be you, as you had to wish to be me. You're just what you said you wanted to be, so you can't complain.'

'It's useless to argue with you, I see,' said Paul. 'And you've no feelings. But I'll warn you of one thing. Whether that is my body or not you've fraudulently taken possession of, I don't know; if it is not, it is very like mine, and I tell you this about it. The sort of life you're leading it, sir, will very soon make an end of you, if you don't take care. Do you think that a constitution at my age can stand sweet wines and pastry, and late hours? Why, you'll be laid up with gout in another day or two. Don't tell me, sir. I know you're suffering from indigestion at this very minute. I can see your liver (it may be my liver for anything I know) is out of order. I can see it in your eyes.'

Dick was a little alarmed at this, but he soon said: 'Well, and if I am seedy, I can get Barbara to take the stone and wish me all right again. Can't I? That's easy enough, I suppose?'

'Oh, easy enough!' said Paul, with a suppressed groan. 'But, Dick, you don't go up to Mincing Lane in that suit and that hat? Don't tell me you do that!'

'When I do go up, I wear them,' said Dick composedly 'Why not? It's a roomy suit, and I hate a great topper on my head; I've had enough of that here on Sundays. But it's slow up at your office. The chaps there aren't half up to any larks. I made a first-rate booby-trap, though, one day for an old yellow buffer who came in to see you. He was in a bait when he found the waste-paper basket on his head!'

'What was his name?' said Paul, with forced calm.

'Something like "Shells." He said he was a very old friend of mine, and I told him he lied.'

'Shellack— my Canton correspondent — a man I was anxious to be of use to when he came over!' moaned Mr Multitude. 'Miserable young cub, you don't know what mischief you've done!'

'Well, it won't matter much to you now,' said Dick; 'you're out of it all.'

'Do you — do you mean to keep me out of it forever then?' asked Paul.

'As long as I ever can!' returned Dick frankly. 'It will be rather interesting to see what sort of a fellow you'll grow into — if you ever do grow. Perhaps you will always be like that, you know. This magic is a rum thing to meddle with.'

There was a pause, in which the conversation seemed about to flag hopelessly, but at last Dick said, almost as if he felt some compunction for his present unfilial attitude: 'Now, you know, it's much better to take things quietly. It can't be altered now, can it? And it's not such bad fun being a boy after all — for some things. You'll get into it by-and-by you see if you don't, and be as jolly as a sand-boy. We shall get along all right together, too. I shan't be hard on you. It is not my fault that you happen to be at this particular

What Happened to a Father Who Became a Schoolboy

school — you chose it! And after this term you can go to any other school you like — Eton or Rugby, or anywhere. I don't mind the expense. Or, if you'd rather, you can have a private tutor. And I'll buy you a pony, and you can ride in the Row. You shall have a much better time of it than I ever had, as long as you let me go on my own way'

But these dazzling bribes had no influence upon Mr Bultitude; nothing short of complete restitution would ever satisfy him, and he was too proud and too angry at his crushing defeat to even pretend to be in the least pacified.

'I don't want your pony' he said bitterly; 'I might as well have a white elephant, and I don't suppose I should enjoy myself much more at a public school than I do here. Let's have no humbug, sir. You're up and I'm down — there's no more to be said — I shall tell the Doctor nothing, but I warn you, if ever the time comes—'

'Oh, of course,' said Dick, feeling tolerably secure, now he had disposed of the main difficulty. 'If you can turn me out, I suppose you will — that's only fair. I shall take care not to give you the chance. And, oh, I say, do you want any tin? How much have you got left?'

Paul turned away his head, lest Dick should see the sudden exultation he knew it must betray, as he said, with an effort to appear unconcerned, 'I came away with exactly five shillings, and I haven't a penny now!'

'I say' said Dick, 'you are a fellow; you must have been going it. How did you get rid of it all in a week?'

'It went, as far as I can understand,' said Mr Bultitude, 'in rabbits and mice. Some boys claimed it as money they paid you to get them, I believe.'

'All your own fault,' said Dick, 'you would have them drowned. But you'd better have some tin to get along with. How much do you want? Will half-a-crown do?'

'Half-a-crown is not much, Dick,' said his father, almost humbly.

School Times

'It's - ahem - a handsome allowance for a young fellow like you,' said Dick, rather unkindly; 'but I haven't any half-crowns left. I must give you this, I suppose.'

And he held out a sovereign, never dreaming what it signified to Paul, who clutched it with feelings too great for words, though gratitude was not. a part of them, for was it not his own money?

And now look out,' said Dick, 'I hear Grim. Remember what I told you; keep it up.'

Dr Grimstone came in with the air of a man who has a painful duty to perform; he started slightly as his eyes noted the change in his visitor's dress and appearance. 'I hope,' he began gravely, 'that your son has spared me the pain of going into the details of his misbehaviour; I wish I could give you a better report of him.'

Dick was plainly, in spite of his altered circumstances, by no means at ease in the schoolmaster's presence; he stood, shifting from foot to foot on the hearthrug, turning extremely red and obstinately declining to raise his eyes from the ground.

'Oh, ah,' he stammered at last, 'you were just going to whack him, weren't you, when I turned up, sir?'

'I found myself forced,' said the Doctor, slightly shocked at this coarse way of putting things, 'to contemplate administering to him (for his ultimate benefit) a sharp corrective in the presence of his school-fellows. I distress you, I see, but the truth must be told. He has no doubt confessed his fault to you?'

'No,' said Dick, 'he hasn't, though. What's he been up to now?'

'I had hoped he would have been more open, more straightforward, when confronted with the father who has proved himself so often indulgent and anxious for his improvement; it would have been a more favourable symptom, I think. Well, I must tell you myself. I know too well what a shock it will be to your scrupulously sensitive moral code, my dear Mr Bultitude (Dick showed a painful inclination to giggle here); but I have to break to

What Happened to a Father Who Became a Schoolboy

you the melancholy truth that I detected this unhappy boy in the act of conducting a secret and amorous correspondence with a young lady in a sacred edifice!'

Dick whistled sharply: 'Oh, I say!' he cried, 'that's bad' (and he wagged his head reprovingly at his disgusted father, who longed to denounce his hypocrisy, but dared not); 'that's bad ... he shouldn't do that sort of thing, you know, should he? At his age too . . . the young dog!'

'This horror is what 1 should have expected from you,' said the Doctor (though he was in truth more than scandalized by the composure with which his announcement was received). Such boldness is indeed characteristic of the dog, an animal which, as you are aware, was with the ancients a synonym for shamelessness. No boy, however abandoned, should hear such words of unequivocal condemnation from a father's lips without a pang of shame!'

Paul was only just able to control his rage by a great effort.

'You're right there, sir,' said Dick; 'he ought to be well ragged for it . . . he'll break my heart, if he goes on like .this, the young beggar. But we musn't be too hard on him, eh? After all, it's nature, you know, isn't it?'

'I beg your pardon?' said Dr Grimstone very stiffly.

'I mean,' explained Dick, with a perilous approach to digging the other in the ribs, 'we did much the same sort of thing in our time, eh? I'm sure I did — lots of times!'

'I can't reproach myself on that head, Mr Bultitude; and permit me to say, that such a tone of treating the affair is apt to destroy the effect, the excellent moral effect, of your most impressively conveyed indignation just now. I merely give you a hint, you understand!'

'Oh, ah,' said Dick, feeling that he had made a mistake, 'yes, I didn't mean that. But I say, you haven't given him a ... a whopping yet, have you?'

'I had just stepped out to procure a cane for that purpose,' said the Doctor, 'when your name was announced.'

'Well, look here, you won't want to start again when I'm gone, will you?'

'An ancient philosopher, my dear sir, was accustomed to postpone the correction of his slaves until the first glow of his indignation had passed away. He found then that he could—'

'Lay it on with more science,' suggested Dick, while Paul writhed where he stood. 'Perhaps so, but you might forgive him now, don't you think? He won't do it again. If he goes writing any more love letters, tell me, and I'll come and talk to him; but he's had a lesson, you know. Let him off this time.'

'I have no right to resist such an entreaty,' said the Doctor, 'though I may be inclined myself to think that a few strokes would render the lesson more permanent. I must ask you to reconsider your plea for his pardon.'

Paul heard this with indescribable anxiety; he had begun to feel tolerably sure that his evil hour was postponed sine die, but might not Dick be cruel and selfish enough to remain neutral, or even side with the enemy, in support of his assumed character?

Luckily he was not. 'I'd rather let him off,' he said awkwardly; 'I don't approve of caning fellows myself. It never did me any good, I know, and I got enough of it to tell.'

'Well, well, I yield. Richard, your father has interceded for you; and I cannot disregard his wishes, though I have my own view in the matter. You will hear no more of this disgraceful conduct, sir, unless you do something to recall it to my memory. Thank your father for his kindness, which you so little deserved, and take your leave of him.'

'Oh, there, it's all right! said Dick; 'he'll behave himself after this, I know. And oh! I say, sir,' he added hastily, 'is - is Dulcie anywhere about?'

'My daughter?' asked the Doctor. 'Would you like to see her?'

What Happened to a Father Who Became a Schoolboy

'I shouldn't mind,' said Dick, blushing furiously.

'I'm sorry to say she has gone out for a walk with her mother,' said the Doctor. 'I'm afraid she cannot be back for some time. It's unfortunate.'

Dick's face fell. 'It doesn't matter,' he muttered awkwardly. 'She's all right, I hope?'

'She is very seldom ailing, I'm happy to say; just now she is particularly well, thank you.'

'Oh, is she?' said Dick gloomily, probably disappointed to find that he was so little missed, and not suspecting that his father had been accepted as a substitute.

'Well, do you mind? Could I see the fellows again for a minute or two. I mean I should rather like to inspect the school, you know.'

'See my boys? Certainly my dear sir, by all means; this way' and he took Dick out to the schoolroom, Paul following out of curiosity. 'You'll find us at our studies, you see,' said the Doctor, as he opened the first baize door. There was a suspicious hubbub and hum of voices from within; but as they entered every boy was bent over his books with the rapt absorption of the devoted student — an absorption that was the direct effect of the sound the door-handle made in turning.

'Our workshop,' said the Doctor airily, looking around. 'My first form, Mr Bultitude. Some good workers here, and some idle ones.'

Dick stood in the doorway, looking (if the truth must be told) uncommonly foolish. He had wanted, in coming there, to enjoy the contrast between the past and present — which accounts for a good many visits of 'old boys' to the scene of their education. But, confronted with his former schoolfellows, he was seized at first with an utterly unreasonable fear of detection.

The class behaved as classes usually do on such occasions. The good boys smirked and the bad ones stared — the general expression being one of uneasy curiosity. Dick never said a word, feeling strangely bashful and nervous.

'This is Tipping, my head boy' touching that young gentleman on the shoulder, and making him several degrees more uncomfortable. 'I expect solid results from Tipping someday.'

'He looks as if his head was pretty solid,' said Dick, who had once cut his knuckles against it.

'My second boy, Biddlecomb. If he applies himself, he top will do me credit in the world.'

'How do you do, Biddlecomb?' said Dick. 'I owe you nine-pence — I mean — oh, hang it, here's a shilling for you! Hallo, Chawner!' he went on, gradually overcoming his first nervousness, 'how are you getting on, eh? Doing much in the sneaking way, lately?'

'You know him!' exclaimed the Doctor with naive surprise.

'No, no; I don't know him. I've heard of him, you know — heard of him!' Chawner looked down his nose with a feeble attempt at a gratified simper, while his neighbours giggled with furtive relish.

'Well,' said Dick at last, after a long look at all the old familiar objects, 'I must be off, you know. Got some important business at home this evening to look after. The fellows look very jolly and content, and all that sort of thing. Enough to make one want to be a boy again almost, eh? Goodbye, you chaps — ahem, young gentlemen, I wish you good morning!'

And he went out, leaving behind him the impression that 'young Bultitude's governor wasn't such a bad old buffer.'

He paused at the open front door, to which Paul and the Doctor had accompanied him. 'Goodbye,' he said.

'I wish I'd seen Dulcie. I should like to see your daughter, sir; but it can't be helped. Goodbye; and you—,' he added in a lower tone to his father, who was standing by, inexpressibly pained and disgusted by his utter want of dignity, 'you mind what I told you. Don't try any games with me!'

And, as he skipped jauntily down the steps to the gateway, the

Doctor followed his unwieldy, oddly dressed form with his eyes, inclining his head gravely to Dick's sweeping wave of the hand, asked with a compassionate tone in his voice, 'You don't happen to know, Richard, my boy, if your father has had any business troubles lately — anything to disturb him?'

And Mr Bultitude's feelings prevented him from making any intelligible reply.

[After more troubles at school, Paul Bultitude runs away, and arrives at his home to find Dick not too happy in the freedom of his strange seniority and about to make an awful mess of things as the paternal man of business. By a strange turn, the Garuda stone is made to perform its magic again; and Paul and Dick become their former selves, father and son -, to their mutual satisfaction.]

— F. Anstey (Guthrie): *Vice Versa (1882).*

Nino Diablo

W.H. Hudson

'Nino Diablo' — the boy-devil — was here, there, and everywhere, helping friends, frustrating foes, turning up where least expected, and vanishing just as mysteriously.

W.H. Hudson, best known for his novel 'Green Mansions', set most of his stories in South America, where he had lived and travelled extensively.

THE WIDE PAMPA ROUGH WITH long grass; a vast level disk now growing dark, the horizon encircling it with a ring as faultless as that made by a pebble dropped into smooth water; above it the clear sky of June, wintry and pale, still showing in the west, the saffron hues of the afterglow tinged with vapoury violet and grey In the centre of the disk a large low rancho thatched with yellow rushes, a few stunted trees and cattle enclosures grouped about it; and dimly seen in the shadows, cattle and sheep reposing. At the gate stands Gregory Gorostiaga, lord of house, lands and ruminating herds, leisurely unsaddling his horse; for whatsoever Gregory does is done with leisure. Although no person is within earshot, he talks much over his task, now rebuking his restive animal, and now cursing his benumbed ringers and the hard knots in his gear. A curse falls readily and not without a certain natural grace from Gregory's lips; it is the oiled feather with which he touches every difficult knot encountered in life. From time to time, he glances towards the open kitchen door, from which issue the far-flaring light of the fire and familiar voices, with savoury smells of cookery that come to his nostrils like pleasant messengers.

The unsaddling over at last, the freed horse gallops away, neighing joyfully to seek his fellows, but Gregory is not four-footed to hurry himself and so, stepping slowly and pausing frequently to look about him as if reluctant to quit the cold night air, he turns towards the house.

The spacious kitchen was lighted by two or three wicks in cups of melted fat, and by a great fire in the middle of the clay floor that cast crowds of dancing shadows on the walls and filled the whole room with grateful warmth. On the walls were fastened many deer's heads, and on their convenient prongs were hung bridles and lassos, ropes of onions and garlic, bunches of dried herbs, and various other objects. At the fire, a piece of beef was roasting on a spit; and in a large pot suspended by hook and chain from the smoke-blackened central beam, boiled and bubbled an ocean of mutton broth, puffing out white clouds of steam redolent of herbs and cumin-seed. Close to the fire, skimmer in hand, sat Magdalen, Gregory's fat and florid wife, engaged in frying pies in a second smaller pot. There also, on a high, straight-backed chair, sat Ascension, her sister-in-law, a wrinkled spinster; also, in a low rush-bottomed seat, her mother-in-law, an ancient white-headed dame, staring blankly into the flames. On the other side of the fire were Gregory's two eldest daughters, occupied just now in serving mate to their elders — that harmless bitter decoction the sipping of which fills up all vacant moments from dawn to bedtime — pretty dove-eyed girls of sixteen, both also named Magdalen, but neither after their mother nor because confusion was loved by the family for its own sake. They were twins, and born on the day sacred to Santa Magdalena. Slumbering dogs and cats were disposed about the floor, along with four children. The eldest, a boy, sitting with legs outstretched before

School Times

him, was cutting threads from a slip of colt's hide looped over his great toe. The two next, boy and girl, were playing a simple game called nines, once known to English children as nine men's morrice; the lines were rudely scratched on the clay floor, and the men they played with were bits of hardened clay, nine red and as many white. The youngest, a girl of five, sat on the floor nursing a kitten that purred contentedly on her lap and drowsily winked its blue eyes at the fire; and as she swayed herself from side to side she lisped out the old lullaby in her baby voice:

> A-ro-ro mi nino,
> A-ro-ro mi sol,
> A-ro-ro pedazos
> De mi corazon.

Gregory stood on the threshold surveying this domestic scene with manifest pleasure.

'Papa mine, what have you brought me?' cried the child with the kitten.

'Brought you, interested? Stiff whiskers and cold hands to pinch your dirty little cheeks. How is your cold tonight, mother?'

'Yes, son, it is very cold tonight; we knew that before you came in,' replied the old dame testily as she drew her chair a little closer to the fire.

'It is useless speaking to her,' remarked Ascension. 'With her to be out of temper is to be deaf.'

'What has happened to put her out?' he asked.

'I can tell you, papa,' cried one of the twins. 'She wouldn't let me make your cigars today, and sat down out of doors to make them herself. It was after breakfast when the sun was warm.'

'And of course she fell asleep,' chimed in Ascension.

'Let me tell it, auntie!' exclaimed the other. 'And she fell asleep, and in a moment Rosita's lamb came and ate up the whole of the tobacco-leaf in her lap.'

Nino Diablo

'It didn't!' cried Rosita, looking up from her game. 'I opened its mouth and looked with all my eyes, and there was no tobacco-leaf in it.'

'That lamb! That lamb!' said Gregory slyly. 'Is it to be wondered at that we are turning grey before our time — all except Rosita! Remind me tomorrow, wife, to take it to the flock; or if it has grown fat on all the tobacco-leaf, aprons and old shoes it has eaten.'

'Oh no, no, no!' screamed Rosita, starting up and throwing the game into confusion, just when her little brother had made a row and was in the act of seizing on one of her pieces in triumph.

'Hush, silly child, he will not harm your lamb,' said the mother, pausing from her task and raising eyes that were tearful with the smoke of the fire and of the cigarette she held between her good-humoured lips. And now, if these children have finished speaking of their important affairs, tell me, Gregory what news do you bring?'

'They say' he returned, sitting down and taking the mate-cup from his daughter's hand, 'that the invading Indians bring seven hundred lances, and that those that first opposed them were all slain. Some say they are now retreating with the cattle they have taken, while others maintain that they are waiting to fight our men.'

'Oh, my sons, my sons, what will happen to them!' cried Magdalen, bursting into tears.

'Why do you cry, wife, before God gives you cause?' returned her husband. 'Are not all men born to fight the infidel? Our boys are not alone — all their friends and neighbours are with them.'

'Say not this to me, Gregory, for I am not a fool nor blind. All their friends indeed! And this the very day I have seen Nino Diablo; he galloped past the house, whistling like a partridge that knows no care. Why must my two sons be called away, while he, a youth

83

without occupation and with no mother to cry for him, remains behind?'

'You talk folly, Magdalen,' replied her lord. 'Complain that the ostrich and puma are more favoured than your sons, since no man calls on them to serve the State; but mention not Nino, for he is freer than the wild things which Heaven has made, and fights not on this side nor On that.'

'Coward! Miserable!' murmured the incensed mother.

Whereupon one of the twins flushed scarlet, and retorted, 'He is not a coward, mother!'

And if not a coward why does he sit on the hearth among women and old men in times like these? Grieved am I to hear a daughter of mine speak in defence of one who is a vagabond and a stealer of other men's horses!'

The girl's eyes flashed angrily, but she answered not a word.

'Hold your tongue, woman, and accuse no man of crimes,' spoke Gregory 'Let every Christian take proper care of his animals; and as for the infidel's horses, he is a virtuous man that steals them. The girl speaks the truth; Nino is no coward, but he fights not with our weapons. The web of the spider is coarse and ill-made compared with the snare he spreads to entangle his prey' Then, fixing his eyes on the face of the girl who had spoken, he added, 'Therefore, be warned in season, my daughter, and fall not into the snare of Nino Diablo.'

Again the girl blushed and hung her head.

At this moment a clatter of hoofs, the jangling of a bell, and cries of a traveller to the horses driven before him, came in at the open door. The dogs roused themselves, almost overturning "the children in their hurry to rush out; and up rose Gregory to find out who was approaching with so much noise.

'I know, *papita*,' cried one of the children. 'It is Uncle Polycarp.'

'You are right, child,' said her father. 'Cousin Polycarp always arrives at night, shouting to his animals like a troop of Indians.' And with that he went out to welcome his boisterous relative.

The traveller soon arrived, spurring his horse, scared at the light and snorting loudly, to within two yards of the door. In a few minutes the saddle was thrown off, the fore feet of the bell-mare fettered, and the horses allowed to wander away in quest of pasturage; then the two men turned into the kitchen.

A short, burly man aged about fifty, wearing a soft hat thrust far back on his head, with truculent greenish eyes beneath arched bushy eyebrows, and a thick shapeless nose surmounting a bristly moustache — such was Cousin Polycarp. From neck to feet he was covered with a blue cloth poncho, and on his heels he wore enormous silver spurs that clanked and jangled over the floor like the fetters of a convict. After greeting the women and bestowing the avuncular blessing on the children, who had clamoured for it as for some inestimable boon, he sat down and flinging back his poncho displayed at his waist a huge silver-hilted knife and a heavy brass-barrelled horse-pistol.

'Heaven be praised for its goodness, Cousin Magdalen,' he said. 'What with pies and spices your kitchen is more fragrant than a garden of flowers. That's as it should be, for nothing but rum have I tasted this bleak day And the boys are away fighting, Gregory tells me. Good! When the eaglets have found out their wings let them try their talons. What, Cousin Magdalen, crying for the boys! Would you have had them girls?'

'Yes, a thousand times,' she replied, drying her wet eyes with her apron.

Ah, Magdalen, daughters can't be always young and sweet-tempered, like your brace of pretty partridges yonder. They grow old, Cousin Magdalen — old and ugly and spiteful; and are more bitter and worthless than the wild pumpkin. But I speak not of those who are present, for I would say nothing to offend my respected Cousin Ascension, whom may God preserve, though she never married.'

'Listen to me, Cousin Polycarp,' returned the insulted dame so pointedly alluded to. 'Say nothing to me nor of me, and I will also hold my peace concerning you; for you know very well that if I were disposed to open my lips I could say a thousand things.'

'Enough, enough, you have already said them a thousand times,' he interrupted. 'I know all that, cousin. Let us say no more.'

'That is only what I ask,' she retorted, 'for I have never loved to bandy words with you and you know already, therefore I need not recall it to your mind, that if I am single it is not because some men whose names I could mention if I felt disposed — and they are the names not of dead but of living men — would not have been glad to marry me; but because I preferred my liberty and the goods I inherited from my father, and I see not what advantage there is in being the wife of one who is a brawler and a drunkard and spender of other people's money, and I know not what besides.'

'There it is!' said Polycarp, appealing to the fire. 'I knew that I had thrust my foot into a red ants' nest — careless that I am! But in truth, Ascension, it was fortunate for you in those distant days you mention that you hardened your heart against all lovers. For wives, like cattle that must be branded with their owner's mark, are first of all taught submission to their husbands and consider, cousin, what tears! What sufferings!' And having ended thus abruptly, he planted his elbows on his knees and busied himself with the cigarette he had been trying to roll up with his cold drunken fingers for the last five minutes.

Ascension gave a nervous twitch at the red cotton handkerchief on her head, and cleared her throat with a sound 'sharp and short like the shrill swallow's cry' when—.

'*Madre del Cielo,* how you frightened me!' screamed one of the twins, giving a great start.

The cause of this sudden outcry was discovered in the presence of a young man quietly seated on the bench at the girl's side. He had not been there a minute before, and no person had seen him enter the room — what wonder that the girl was startled! He was slender in form, and had small hands and feet, and oval olive face, smooth as a girl except for the incipient moustache on his lip. In place of a hat he wore only a scarlet ribbon bound about his head, to keep back the glossy black hair that fell to his shoulders; and he was wrapped in a white woolen Indian poncho, while his lower limbs were cased in white colt-skin coverings, shaped like stockings to his feet, with the red tassels of his embroidered garters falling to the ankles.

'Nino Diablo!' all cried in a breath, the children manifesting the greatest joy at his appearance. But old Gregory spoke with affected anger. 'Why do you always drop on us in such a treacherous way like rain through a leaky thatch?' he exclaimed. 'Keep these strange arts for your visits in the infidel country; here we are all Christians, and praise God on the threshold when we visit a neighbour's house. And now, Nino Diablo, what news of the Indians?'

'Nothing do I know and little do I concern myself about specks on the horizon,' returned the visitor with a light laugh. And at once all the children gathered around him, for Nino they considered to belong to them when he came, and not to their elders with their solemn talk about Indian warfare and lost horses. And now, he would finish that wonderful story, long in the telling, of the little girl alone and lost in the great desert, and surrounded by all the wild animals met to discuss what they should do with her. It was a grand story, even mother Magdalen listened to it carefully, though she pretended all the tune to be thinking only of her pies — and the teller, like the grand old historians of other days, put most eloquent

School Times

speeches, all made out of his own head, into the lips (and beaks) of the various actors — puma, ostrich, deer, cavy and the rest.

In the midst of this performance supper was announced, and all gathered willingly round a dish of Magdalen's pies, filled with minced meat, chopped hard-boiled eggs, raisins, and plenty if spice. After the pies came roast beef and finally, great basins of mutton broth fragrant with herbs and cumin seed. After the rage of hunger satisfied each one said a prayer, the elders murmuring with bowed heads, the children on their knees uplifting shrill voices. Then followed the concluding semi-religious ceremony of the day, when each child in its turn asked a blessing of father, mother, grandmother, uncle, aunt, and not omitting the stranger within the gates, even Nino Diablo of evil-sounding name.

The men drew forth their pouches, and began making their cigarettes, when once more the children gathered around the storyteller, their faces glowing with expectation.

'No, no,' cried their mother. 'No more stories tonight — to bed, to bed!'

'Oh, mother, mother!' cried Rosita pleadingly and struggling to free herself; for the good woman had dashed in among them to enforce obedience. 'Oh, let me stay till the story ends! The reed-cat has said such things! Oh, what will they do with the poor little girl?'

'And oh, mother mine!' drowsily sobbed her little sister, 'the armadillo that said — that said nothing because it had nothing to say, and the partridge that whistled and said—' and here she broke into a prolonged wail. The boys also added their voices until the hubbub was no longer to be borne, and Gregory rose up in his wrath and called on someone to lend him a big whip; only then they yielded, and still sobbing and casting many a lingering look behind, were led from the kitchen.

During this scene Nino had been carrying on a whispered conversation with the pretty Magdalen of his choice, heedless of the uproar of which he had been the indirect cause; deaf also to the bitter remarks of Ascension concerning some people who, having no homes of their own, were fond of coming uninvited into other people's houses, only to repay the hospitality extended to them by stealing their silly daughters' affections, and teaching their children to rebel against their authority.

But the noise and confusion had served to arouse Polycarp from a drowsy fit; for, like a boa-constrictor, he had dined largely after his long fast, and dinner had made him dull; bending towards his cousin he whispered earnestly: 'Who is this young stranger, Gregory?'

'In what corner of the earth have you been hiding to ask who Nino Diablo is?' returned the other.

'Must I know the history of every cat and dog?'

'Nino is neither a cat nor a dog, cousin, but a man among men, like a falcon among birds. When a child of six, the Indians killed all his relations and carried him into captivity. After five years he escaped out of their hands, and guided by sun and stars and signs on the earth, he found his way back to the Christians' country, bringing many beautiful horses stolen from his captors; also the name of Nino Diablo, first given to him by the infidel. We know him by no other.'

'This is a good story; in truth I like it well — it pleases me mightily' said Polycarp. 'And what more, Cousin Gregory?'

'More than I can tell, cousin. When he comes the dogs do not bark — who knows why? His tread is softer than the cat's; the untamed horse is tame for him. Always in the midst of dangers, yet no harm, no scratch. Why? Because he stoops like the falcon, makes his stroke and is gone — Heaven knows where!'

'What strange things are you telling me? Wonderful! And what more, Cousin Gregory?'

'He often goes into the Indian country, and lives freely with the infidel, disguised, for they do not know him who was once their captive. They speak of Nino Diablo to him, saying that when they

School Times

catch that thief they will flay him alive. He listens to their strange stories, then leaves them, taking their finest ponchos and silver ornaments, and the flower of their horses.'

A brave youth, one after my own heart, Cousin Gregory. Heaven defends and prospers him in all his journeys into the Indian Territory! Before we part I shall embrace him and offer him my friendship, which is worth something. More, tell me more, Cousin Gregory!'

'These things I am telling you to put you on your guard; look well to your horses, cousin.'

'What!' shouted the other, lifting himself up from his stooping posture, and staring at his relation with astonishment and kindling, anger in his countenance.

The conversation had been carried on in a low tone, and the sudden loud exclamation startled them all — all except Nino, who continued smoking and chatting pleasantly to the twins.

'Lightning and pestilence, what is this you say to me, Gregory Gorostiaga!' continued Polycarp, violently slapping his thigh and thrusting his hat farther back on his head.

'Prudence!' whispered Gregory. 'Say nothing to offend Nino, he never forgives an enemy — with horses.'

'Talk not to me of prudence!' bawled the other. 'You hit me on the apple of the eye and counsel me not to cry out. What! Have not I, whom men call Polycarp of the south, wrestled with tigers in the desert, and must I hold my peace because of a boy — even a boy-devil? Talk of what you like, cousin, and I am a meek man -meek as a sucking babe; but touch not on my horses, for then I am a whirlwind, a conflagration, a river flooded in winter, and all wrath and destruction like an invasion of Indians! Who can stand before me? Ribs of steel are no protection! Look at my knife; do you ask why there are stains on the blade? Listen, because it has gone straight to the robber's heart!' And with that he drew out his great knife and nourished it wildly, and made stabs and slashes at an imaginary foe suspended above the fire.

The pretty girls grew silent and pale and trembled like poplar leaves; the old grandmother rose up, and clutching at her shawl toddled hurriedly away, while Ascension uttered a snort of disdain. But Nino still talked and smiled, blowing thin smoke-clouds from his lips, careless of that tempest of wrath gathering before him; till, seeing the others so calm, the man of war returned his weapon to its sheath, and glancing around and lowering his voice to a conversational tone informed his listeners that his name was Polycarp, one known and feared by all men — especially in the south; that he was disposed to live in peace and amity with the entire human race, and he therefore considered it unreasonable of some men to follow him about the world asking him to kill them. 'Perhaps,' he concluded, with a touch of irony 'they think I gain something by putting them to death. A mistake, good friends; I gain nothing by it! I am not a vulture, and their dead bodies can be of no use to me.'

Just after this sanguinary protest and disclaimer, Nino, all at once, made a gesture as if to impose silence, and turned his face towards the door, his nostrils dilating, and his eyes appearing to grow large and luminous like those of a cat.

'What do you hear, Nino?' asked Gregory.

'I hear lapwings screaming,' he replied.

'Only at a fox perhaps,' said the other. 'But go to the door, Nino, and listen.'

'No need,' he returned, dropping his hand, the light of a sudden excitement passing from his face. 'Tis only a single horseman riding this way at a fast gallop.'

Polycarp got up and went to the door, saying that when a man was among robbers it behaved him to look well after his cattle. Then he came back and sat down again. 'Perhaps,' he remarked, with a

School Times

side glance at Nino, 'a better plan would be to watch the thief. A lie, Cousin Gregory; no lapwings are screaming; no single horseman approaching at a fast gallop. The night is serene, and earth as silent as the sepulcher.'

'Prudence!' whispered Gregory again. 'Ah, cousin, always playful like a kitten; when will you grow old and wise? Can you not see a sleeping snake without turning aside to stir it up with your naked foot?'

Strange to say, Polycarp made no reply. A long experience in getting up quarrels had taught him that these impassive men were, in truth, often enough like venomous snakes, quick and deadly when roused. He became secret and watchful in his manner.

All now were intently listening. Then said Gregory, 'Tell us, Nino, what voices, fine as the trumpet of the smallest fly do you hear coming from that great silence? Has the mother skunk put her little ones to sleep in their kennel and gone out to seek for the pipit's nest? Have fox and armadillo met to challenge each other to fresh trials of strength and cunning? What is the owl saying at this moment to his mistress in praise of her big green eyes?'

The young man smiled slightly but answered nothing; and for full five minutes all listened, then sounds of approaching hoofs became audible. Dogs began to bark, horses began to snort in alarm, and Gregory rose and went forth to receive the late night-wanderer. Soon he appeared, beating the angry barking dogs off with his whip, a white-faced, wild-haired man, furiously spurring his horse like a person demented or flying from robbers.

'Ave Maria! he shouted aloud and when the answer was given in suitable pious words, the scared-looking stranger drew near, and bending down said, 'Tell me, good friend, is one whom men call Nino Diablo with you, for to this house I have been directed in my search for him?'

'He is within, friend,' answered Gregory. 'Follow me and you shall see him with your own eyes. Only first unsaddle, so that your horse may roll before the sweat dries on him.'

'How many horses have I ridden their last journey on this quest!' said the stranger, hurriedly pulling off the saddle and rugs. 'But tell me one thing more; is he well — no indisposition? Has he met with no accident—a broken bone, a sprained ankle?'

'Friend,' said Gregory, 'I have heard that once in past times the moon met with an accident, but of Nino no such thing has been reported to me.'

With this assurance the stranger followed his host into the kitchen, made his salutation, and sat down by the fire. He was about thirty years old, a good-looking man, but his face was haggard, his eyes bloodshot, his manner restless, and he appeared like one half-crazed by some great calamity. The hospitable Magdalen placed food before him and pressed him to eat. He complied, although reluctantly, dispatched his supper in a few moments, and murmured a prayer; then, glancing curiously at the two men seated near him, he addressed himself to the burly well-armed, and dangerous-looking Polycarp. 'Friend,' he said, his agitation increasing as he spoke, 'four days have I been seeking you, taking neither food nor rest, so great was my need of your assistance. You alone, after God, can help me. Help me in this strait, and half of all I possess in land and cattle and gold shall be freely given to you, and the angels above will applaud your deed!'

'Drunk or mad?' was the only reply vouchsafed to this appeal.

'Sir,' said the stranger with dignity, 'I have not tasted wine these many days, nor has my great grief crazed me.'

'Then what ails the man?' said Polycarp. 'Fear perhaps; for he is white in the face like one who has seen the Indians.'

'In truth I have seen them. I was one of those unfortunates who first opposed them, and most of the friends who were with me are now food for wild dogs. Where our houses stood, there are only

School Times

ashes and a stain of blood on the ground. Oh, friend, can you not guess why you alone were in my thoughts when this trouble came to me — why I have ridden day and night to find you?

'Demons!' exclaimed Polycarp, 'into what quagmires would this man lead me? Once for all, I understand you not! Leave me in peace, strange man, or we shall quarrel.' And here he tapped his weapon significantly.

At this juncture, Gregory, who took his time about everything, thought proper to interpose. 'You are mistaken, friend,' he said.

'The young man sitting on your right is Nino Diablo, for whom you inquired a little while ago.'

A look of astonishment, followed by one of intense relief came over the stranger's face. Turning to the young man he said, 'My friend, forgive me this mistake. Grief has perhaps dimmed my sight; but sometimes the iron blade and the blade of finest temper are not easily distinguished by the eyes. When we try them we know which is the brute metal, and cast it aside to take up the other, and trust our life to it. The words I have spoken were meant for you, and you have heard them.'

'What can I do for you, friend?' said Nino.

'Oh, sir, the greatest service! You can restore my lost wife to me. The savages have taken her away into captivity. What can I do to save her — I, who cannot make myself invisible, and fly like the wind, and compass all things?' And here he bowed his head, and covering his face gave way to over-mastering grief.

'Be comforted, friend,' said the other, touching him lightly on the arm. 'I will restore her to you.'

'Oh, friend, how shall I thank you for these words? cried the unhappy man, seizing and pressing Nino's hand.

'Tell me her name — describe her to me.'

'Torcuata is her name — Torcuata de la Rosa. She is one finger's width taller than this young woman,' indicating one of the twins who was standing.

Nino Diablo

'But not dark; her cheeks are rosy — no, no, I forget, they will be pale now, whiter than the grass plumes, with stains of dark colour under the eyes. Brown hair and blue eyes, but very deep blue. Look well, friend, lest you think them black and leave her to perish.'

'Never!' remarked Gregory, shaking his head.

'Enough, you have told me enough, friend,' said Nino, rolling up a cigarette.

'Enough!' repeated the other, surprised. 'But you do not know; she is my life; my life is in your hands. How can I persuade you to be with me? I had gone to pay the herdsmen their wages when the Indians came unexpectedly; and my house at La Chilca, on the banks of the Langueyú, was burnt, and my wife taken away during my absence. Eight hundred head of cattle have escaped the savages, and half of them shall be yours; and half of all I possess in money and land.'

'Cattle!' returned Nino smiling, and holding a lighted stick to his cigarette. 'I have enough to eat without molesting myself with the care of cattle.'

'But I told you that I had other things,' said the stranger full of distress.

The young man laughed, and rose from his seat.

'Listen to me,' he said. 'I go now to follow the Indians — to mix with them, perhaps. They are retreating slowly, burdened with much spoil. In fifteen days, go to the little town of Tandil, and wait for me there. As for land, if God has given so much of it to the ostrich it is not a thing for a man to set a great value on.' Then he bent down to whisper a few words in the ear of the girl at his side; and immediately afterwards, with a simple 'good night' to the others, stepped lightly from the kitchen. By another door the girl also hurriedly left the room, to hide her tears from the watchful censuring eyes of mother and aunt.

Then the stranger, recovering from his astonishment at the

School Times

abrupt ending of the conversation, started up, and crying aloud, 'Stay! Stay one moment, one word more!' rushed out after the young man. At some distance from the house he caught sight of Nino, sitting motionless on his horse, as if waiting to speak to him.

'This is what I have to say to you,' spoke Nino, bending down to the other. 'Go back to Langueyú, and rebuild your house, and expect me there with your wife in about thirty days. When I bade you go to the Tandil in fifteen days, I spoke only to mislead that man Polycarp, who has an evil mind. Can I ride a hundred leagues and back in fifteen days? Say no word of this to any man. And fear not. If I fail to return with your wife at the appointed time, take some of that money you have offered me, and bid a priest say a mass for my soul's repose; for eyes of man shall never see me again, and the brown hawks will be complaining that there is no more flesh to be picked from my bones.'

During this brief colloquy, and afterwards, when Gregory and his women-folk went off to bed, leaving the stranger to sleep in his rugs beside the kitchen fire, Polycarp, who had sworn a mighty oath not to close his eyes that night, busied himself making his horses secure. Driving them home, he tied them to the posts of the gate within twenty-five yards of the kitchen door. Then he sat down by the fire and smoked and dozed, and cursed his dry mouth and drowsy eyes that were so hard to keep open. At intervals of about fifteen minutes he would get up and go out to satisfy himself that his precious horses were still safe. At length in rising, sometime after midnight, his foot kicked against some loud-sounding metal object lying beside him on the floor, which on examination proved to be a copper bell of a peculiar shape, and curiously like the one fastened to the neck of his bell-mare. Bell in hand, he stepped to the door and put out his head, and lo! His horses were no longer at the gate! Eight horses: seven iron-grey geldings, every one of them swift and sure-footed, sound as the bell in his hand, and as like each other as seven claret-coloured eggs in the tinamu's nest; and the eighth the gentle piebald mare — the *madrina* his horses loved and would follow to the world's end, now, alas! With a thief on her back! Gone, gone!

He rushed out, uttering a succession of frantic howls and imprecations; and finally, to wind up the performance, dashed the now useless bell with all his energy against the gate, shattering it into a hundred pieces. Oh, that bell, how often and how often in how many a wayside public-house had he boasted, in his cups and when sober, of its mellow, far-reaching tone — the sweet sound that assured him in the silent watches of the night that his beloved steeds were safe! Now he danced on the broken fragments, digging them into the earth with his heel; now in his frenzy he could have dug them up again to grind them to powder with his teeth!

The children turned restlessly in bed, dreaming of the lost little girl in the desert; and the stranger half awoke, muttering, 'Courage, O Torcuata — let not your heart break . . . Soul of my life, he gives you back to me — on my bosom, *rosa fresca, rosa fresca!*' Then the hands unclenched themselves again, and the muttering died away. But Gregory awoke fully and instantly divined the cause of the clamour. 'Magdalen! Wife!' he said. 'Listen to Polycarp; Nino has paid him out for his insolence! Oh fool, I warned him, and he would not listen!' But Magdalen refused to wake; and so, hiding his head under the coverlet, he made the bed shake with suppressed laughter, so pleased was he at the clever trick played on his blustering cousin. All at once his laughter ceased, and popped out his head again, showing in the dim light a somewhat long and solemn face. For he had suddenly thought of his pretty daughter asleep in the adjoining room. Asleep! Wide awake, more likely, thinking of her sweet lover, brushing the dews from the hoary pampas grass in his southward flight, speeding away into the heart of the vast mysterious wilderness. Listening also to her uncle, the desperado, apostrophizing the midnight stars; while with his knife he excavates two deep trenches, three yards long and intersecting each other at right angles — a sacred symbol on which he intends, when finished, to swear a most horrible vengeance. 'Perhaps,' muttered Gregory, 'Nino has still other pranks to play in this house.'

When the stranger heard next morning what had happened, he was better able to understand Nino's motive in giving him that caution overnight; nor was he greatly put out, but thought it better that an evil-minded man should lose his horses than that Nino should set out badly mounted on such an adventure:

'Let me not forget,' said the robbed man, as he rode away on a horse borrowed from his cousin, 'to be at the Tandil this day fortnight, with a sharp knife and a blunderbuss charged with a handful of powder and not fewer than twenty-three slugs.'

Terribly in earnest was Polycarp of the South! He was there at the appointed time, slugs and all; but the smooth-cheeked, mysterious, child-devil came not; nor, stranger still, did the scared-looking de la Rosa come clattering in to look for his lost Torcuata. At the end of the fifteenth day, de la Rosa was at Langueyú; seventy-five miles from the Tandil, alone in his new rancho, which had just been rebuilt with the aid of a few neighbours. Through all that night he sat alone by the fire, pondering many things. If he could only recover his lost wife, then he would bid a long farewell to that wild frontier and take her across the great sea, and to that old tree-shaded stone farmhouse in Andalusia, which he had left when he was a boy, and where his aged parents still lived, thinking no more to see their wandering son. His resolution was taken; he would sell all he possessed, all except a portion of land in the Langueyú with the house he had just rebuilt; and to Nino Diablo, the deliverer, he would say, 'Friend, though you despise the things that others value, take this land and poor house for the sake of the girl, Magdalen, you love; for then perhaps her parents will no longer deny her to you.'

He was still thinking of these things, when a dozen or twenty military starlings — that cheerful scarlet-breasted songster of the lonely pampas — alighted on the thatch outside, and warbling their gay, careless winter-music told him that it was day. And all day long, on foot and on horseback, his thoughts were of his lost Torcuata; and when evening once more drew near, his heart was sick with suspense and longing; and climbing the ladder placed against the gable of his rancho he stood on the roof gazing westwards into the blue distance. The sun, crimson and large, sunk into the great green sea of grass, and from all the plain rose the tender fluting notes of the tinamu-partridges, bird answering bird. 'Oh, that I could pierce the haze with my vision,' he murmured, 'that I could see across a hundred leagues of level plain, and look this moment on your sweet face, Torcuata!'

And Torcuata was in truth a hundred leagues distant from him at that moment; and if the miraculous sight he wished for had been given, this was what he would have seen. A wide barren plain scantily clothed with yellow tufts of grass and thorny shrubs, and at its southern extremity, shutting out the view on that side, a low range of dune-like hills. Over this level ground, towards the range, moves a vast herd of cattle and horses — fifteen or twenty thousand head — followed by a scattered horde of savages armed with their long lances. In a small compact body in the centre ride the captives, women and children. Just as the red orb touches the horizon the hills are passed, and lo! A wide grassy valley beyond, with flocks and herds pasturing, and scattered trees, and the blue gleam of water from a chain of small lakes! There, full in sight, is the Indian settlement, the smoke rising peacefully up from the clustered huts. At the sight of home the savages burst into loud cries of joy and triumph, answered, as they drew near, with piercing screams of welcome from the village population, chiefly composed of women, children and old men.

It is past midnight; the young moon has set; the last fires are dying down; the shouts and loud noise of excited talk and laughter have ceased, and the weary warriors, after feasting on sweet mare's flesh to repletion, have fallen asleep in their huts, or, lying out of doors on the ground. Only the dogs are excited still and keep up an incessant barking. Even the captive women, huddled together in one hut in the middle of the settlement, fatigued with their long rough journey, have cried themselves to sleep at last.

At length one of the sad sleepers wakes, or half wakes, dreaming that someone has called her name. How could such a thing be? Yet her own name still seems ringing in her brain, and at length, fully awake, she finds herself intently listening. Again it sounded 'Torcuata' — a voice fine as the pipe of a mosquito, yet so sharp and distinct that it tingled in her ear. She sat up and listened again, and once more it sounded, 'Torcuata!' 'Who speaks?' she returned in a fearful whisper. The voice, still fine and small, replied, 'Come out from among the others until you touch the wall.' Trembling she obeyed, creeping out from among the sleepers until she came into contact with the side of the hut. Then the voice sounded again, 'Creep round the wall until you come to a small crack of light on the other side. Again she obeyed, and when she reached the line of faint light it widened quickly to an aperture, through which a shadowy arm was passed round her waist; and in a moment she was lifted up, and saw the stars above her, and at her feet dark forms of men wrapped in their ponchos lying asleep. But no one woke, no alarm was given; and in a very few minutes she was mounted, man-fashion, on a bare-backed horse, speeding swiftly over the dim plains, with the shadowy form of her mysterious deliverer some yards in advance, driving before him a score or so of horses. He had only spoken half a dozen words to her since their escape from the hut, but she knew by those words that he was taking her to Langueyú.

Undershorts and Roses

Muzaffer Izgu

A story from Turkey.
'All my classmates and the teacher were staring at me.'
What it means to be poor in a school full of affluent children . . .

MY FATHER DIDN'T WANT ME to attend school, but mother very much wanted me to go to school. Father got angry with her.

'How can I look after my family of six in this city? Let him work too. What will he do if he goes to middle school anyway? Let him peddle sesame buns or stuffed clams. How much money does Shahan's son make a day, after all!' he said.

Mother always quoted our teacher in the village.

'Didn't Cebbar Bey say to educate this boy, because he has a good head?' she said.

Father yelled, 'Middle school is very expensive, costs lots of money!'

Mother replied softly, 'I'll economize, reduce expenses.'

This was why if one of the teachers at school said, 'You need this kind of notebook, that kind of file cover or such and such atlas,' my heart skipped a beat. It cost so much money for notebooks, file folders, pencils . . . especially my books. . . . when mother asked for five hundred lira, my father yelled his head off.

'So he goes to school. So what will he be?' he shouted.

'He'll be a man,' my mother answered.

The atlas, that big book with the maps, it cost a fortune. Mother was amazed and so was I. And those two-hundred page notebooks the mathematics teacher required . . . Good grief! That's how most of the five hundred lira went.

My music teacher said, 'Flute.'

I couldn't get one. If students could get one, it was fine. Our teacher gave lessons. Then they could get the top grade, 'ten' in music, especially if they played their flutes together and made our school proud at the evening entertainment.

My friends obtained them, something like a shepherd's pipe, but I couldn't buy one. 'Let them give me an average grade of 'five.' I'll memorise *do re mi* and recite it to the teacher,' I said to myself. Anyway, the teacher didn't force everyone to buy one, only those who wished to.

But our physical education teacher didn't say, 'Let those who wish get them.'

He said, 'I'll see you all in shorts in one week.'

Shorts! I didn't know what sort of thing shorts were!

Our teacher added, 'If I see anyone without shorts at the end of the week, don't blame me for what happens!'

The second class, in talking about the physical education teacher, said, 'Uhuu, he'll even beat you up. . . .'

I was afraid. At the break, I asked the schoolmate who sat beside me. He said that shorts are like underpants, short underpants. . . . Girls wear white shorts, boys black. Physical education classes mean discipline. Discipline first begins with what you wear, that is, black shorts. In addition to the black shorts, you have a jersey. They don't like coloured jerseys; they have to be pure white.

He told me that right now we'll take our physical education class in shorts, because the weather is good, but when it gets cold, we'll have to wear sweatsuits. The sweatsuits are navy blue. The best ones are wool but, if you're short of money, you can get nylon or cotton.

The physical education teacher's last words before class ended were: Anyone who doesn't come to my class properly dressed, can't get a good grade from me!'

When I came home, I told my mother. She told father that evening. Again, he got angry.

'I can't give you a nickel for ten days because I don't get paid until then.'

Mother patted my head. 'Tell your teacher,' she said, 'tell him you'll wear them next week.'

Sadik Bey won't accept it... Not only that, he'll beat me. Didn't the second class say, 'If he gets angry, he'll beat you?'

'He'll beat me, mother,' I whispered.

'He won't raise a big fuss for just one week, son. Don't they know what poverty is?' 'I don't know....'

My mother doesn't buy cloth especially for sewing our underpants. She makes them from whatever cloth is available. Actually, I have two pairs of underpants, one I wear while my mother washes the other. One is made from leftover quilt material, the other from the print curtains on the windows of our shanty. These second ones have large roses on them.

Well, what if the teacher said that day, 'Seeing you don't have any shorts, take off your trousers and participate in your underpants.' Then I'd be dressed in those rose print shorts.

I asked mother about it.

'No,' she said. 'Why should he say anything? He's going to have you run, so let him have you run in trousers!'

What if I didn't go to school that day? Mother would be angry. I had promised her I would never cut school.

She had told me, 'Look son, your father doesn't want you to go to school. If he hears you bunked school, he'll scold me and give me a real dressing-down. So I beg you, never run away from school. Bring home such a good report card, such good grades, that we can show your father that you really should be in school.'

'I promise, mother, I promise,' I said.

I won't go back on my word, especially on a promise made to my mother.

One day there was a physical education class scheduled. All the Other kids said that they had their shorts and jerseys. But Ilyas and I said nothing. Ilyas, like me, came from a shanty town to go to school.

During the break, I asked Ilyas and he said, 'I couldn't get them. I'll participate in trousers.'

'Me, too,' I replied.

I had taken strength from there being two of us. I wasn't by myself anymore. When we had to line up for the physical education class and the class leader made his report, 'Class-One-A is ready for physical education,' I wouldn't be the only one in trousers among all those in shorts and jerseys; there would be Ilyas, too. Who knows, maybe other boys also... Then our teacher, Sadik Bey, wouldn't say anything.

The second period passed.

The third period passed.

The fourth period passed, too.

Four classes and everything went in one ear and out the other. In the fifth and sixth periods, I thought of nothing but that physical education class. I thought of Sadik Bey's muscular arms and frowning eyebrows.

The bell rang and all of us boys went outside. First the girls were to get dressed. The boys gathered around the door. Once in a while they knocked and yelled:

'Hurry up in there; the bell's about to ring!'

Girls' voices came from inside:

'Don't open the door, just don't open it; we're getting dressed!' they squealed.

The girls came out. They had become like white butterflies in

Undershorts and Roses

their white blouses and shorts. Running through the crowd of boys, they flew to the yard, to the field where the physical education class was held. Then the boys crowded in. Only Ilyas and I didn't go in. The two of us leaned against the wall beside the classroom door and looked about us with scared eyes. We didn't know what Sadik Bey was going to do to us.

Ilyas asked. 'Shall we run away?'

'No,' I answered.

'But what if he hits us!'

The bell rang. Our classmates in their black shorts and white jerseys ran past us, one by one.

'How about you?' our class leader asked. 'We haven't any' we replied. 'Hurry to the lineup!'

We ran. The girls were lined up on one side, the boys on the other according to height. Ilyas and I lined up at the far rear. The class leader, roll book in hand, waited for our physical education teacher. Both boys and girls twittered noisily. Only two of us, Ilyas and I, remained silent.

Soon Sadik Bey appeared at the schoolhouse door in his red sweatsuit. We saw him twirling his whistle on a chain with one hand, as he always did.

'Hurry, line up, he's coming!' our leader yelled.

The girls and boys formed up, the twittering stopped and they were lined up like a rope.

He's coming! Ten steps later he was beside us.

'Rest, attentiooon!'

We came to attention.

Our leader yelled, 'Class-One-A prepared for physical education class, teacher!'

Sadik Bey called, 'Good day!'

We replied, 'Thank yoooooou!'

Before signing the rollbook, Sadik Bey's eyes fell on us. He told

School Times

the class leader, 'I see that Class-One-A is not prepared for physical education.'

He pointed at us, and then motioned for us to come forward. Ilyas and I ran to the teacher.

'How about your shorts and jerseys?'

'My father didn't get paid, teacher,' I explained.

'Well, well, so when he does get paid he's going to buy a yacht or something?' He yelled, 'Shorts and jersey, how much are they, after all?'

'I don't know, teacher.'

'Run, go and take off your jacket and trousers.'

It was then that my breath caught and I started to feel faint. Ilyas had run off but I couldn't seem to move. All my classmates and the teacher were staring at me.

'Come on. I told you to go. Run quickly!'

At this point he signed the roll book. When he saw me standing motionless in my tracks, he said, 'Don't you understand me, you?'

I understand, I thought to myself, but I wonder if my comrades will understand the situation? Won't they laugh when I come out in my rose-print underpants; won't they make fun of me?

He grabbed me by the hair. 'Run, I told you!' he yelled.

I couldn't run. It seemed such a short distance between the field and the schoolhouse, like only two steps. The hall, the corridor like one little step.

'Pssst!' said Uyas.

I hardly saw his gray underpants as he flew off to the field. I entered the classroom, took off my jacket and put it in my desk cubbyhole. I took off my shirt and put it in, too. I just couldn't make my hands unbutton my trousers.

But . . . Sadik Bey had yelled after me, 'We're waiting for you, hurry!'

They were waiting for me. All my classmates were waiting for

Undershorts and Roses

me. They were waiting to see my rose-print underpants. I know, now their eyes are on the school door. When I come out in those rose-print underpants, neither Sadik Bey nor discipline will suppress their laughter.

I considered grabbing my schoolbag and running home, but no, I had promised my mother. I was going to make her proud. I unbuttoned my trousers and took them off. The window curtains from our shanty were revealed. Above my legs, enormous red roses and among them, purple leaves. Right over my navel was a rosebud. I don't know how they looked in back.

I left the classroom and walked along close to the wall. I was scared to death that a door would open and someone would come out. But what about when I came into the yard or reached the steps? They were waiting for me there. Sadik Bey was waiting. If only he had taken me to one side before he had said, 'Go and take off your trousers!' and asked, I would have told him, I'm embarrassed; they have roses on them. . . .' Then if he'd said, 'In that case don't participate in the class today; watch us from the sidelines. . . .' If only, oh if only. . .

This time, the way from the school building to the field seemed longer. I walked and walked but it seemed never ending. I couldn't look up at my comrades; my eyes were fixed on the ground. But I heard the laughs. The laughing gradually got louder until all the boys and girls were laughing. Our teacher said nothing to them. I approached him and raised my head and saw that he was laughing, too. One phrase came from my teacher's mouth, 'Fashion show!' he said.

After that remark, my classmates laughed even louder. Then, I even forgot the promise I made to my mother. Suddenly, I began to run. The teacher blew his whistle at me but I ran right outside the school gate in those underpants.

But, but . . . What had my mother told me?

School Times

'Always insist on your rights,' she'd said.

I turned back, hurried into the schoolhouse and up to the second floor. I was crying; my eyes full of tears. . . My physical education teacher hadn't tried to stop my classmates from laughing at me; he even laughed himself. In that case, to whom should I make a complaint? To the principal ... To the school principal.

I knocked on his door and went inside...I couldn't talk because of my hard sobs.

I could say, 'Aaa, they mocked me.'

The principal stood up and came to me. He took my arm and sat me in a chair.

'Tell me about it, my son.'

'Under . . . they made fun of my underpants,' I sobbed. 'Both the teacher and my friends were making fun . . .'

He pressed a bell and the office boy came. He asked me which desk my trousers were in. I told him. In a moment, the office boy came with my schoolbag and clothes. The principal himself dressed me and handed me my schoolbag.

'All right, my son, you're off for the rest of the day. Go home!'

At the next physical education class, I had my black shorts and white jersey. Sadik Bey didn't beat me because I ran away But I will never like him. I'm still so angry inside that I can never forgive him.

–Reprinted from Short Story International (Student Series)

Til Eulenspiegel's Merry Pranks

Nothing is known of the author of Til Eulenspiegel, a collection of light-hearted tales popular in Germany even before they were collected as one work in the fifteenth century. Our mischievous young hero is central to all of them.

IN THE TOWN OF HERDELLEM there lived a rich merchant. One morning, while he was walking through his fields, he saw a youth lying idly on the grass. A lanky-looking fellow he was, with shabby clothes and a long, solemn face. The merchant sauntered up to him, and asked his name, and why he was idling there when everybody else was at work.

'My name is Til Eulenspiegel,' answered the youth. As for work, I have none. I am a cook who has lost his master.'

A cook!' said the merchant. 'That's good! You're the very man I'm looking for!'

'My master was a cook, too,' went on Eulenspiegel.

'How's that? You were cook to a cook?'

'Yes, sir. I was a kitchen-boy.'

The merchant smiled when he heard this. 'Well, if you come along with me,' he said, 'I will turn you into a real cook, and give you good wages into the bargain. In any case, there's no harm in giving you a try; my wife is always quarrelling with her cooks.'

'Cheerful news,' thought Eulenspiegel, but he said nothing.

'Come along, then,' went on the merchant. 'Let us go off to my

School Times

garden and gather herbs to boil with the young spring chickens, for I am having a big party tomorrow, and I want everything to be of the best.'

'You can rely on me,' said Eulenspiegel, and they went off together to the merchant's house.

'What's this? Another servant?' said the merchant's wife to her husband when she saw them coming. 'I suppose you think we have more food than we know what to do with!'

'Don't fret yourself, my dear,' rejoined the merchant. 'This is the very man we want. Come with me, lad,' he went on to Eulenspiegel, 'and help me fetch the meat for tomorrow'

They went down to the meat market, and bought two huge pieces of meat. One was for boiling, and the other was for roasting on a spit over the fire. 'When you cook these tomorrow,' said the merchant, 'be sure to put on the boiling piece pretty early, so that it may have a long time to cook. As for the roast, keep it some distance from the flames and don't let it get too hot, or it will singe and burn.'

'Very good, master,' said Til Eulenspiegel. 'I will do exactly as you say.'

The next day he put the boiling joint on early, as he had been told to do; but the beef he stuck on a spit and placed in the cellar, hanging between two barrels of beer. Before the guests had all assembled, the merchant came to the kitchen to see that the meal was ready. (His wife was far too grand a lady ever to come into the kitchen at all.) 'Well now,' he inquired, 'is everything ready?'

'Everything is cooked,' answered Eulenspiegel, 'except the roast beef.'

'Everything but the roast beef!' exclaimed the merchant. 'And what has happened to that?'

'It is on a spit in the cellar,' answered the new cook. 'You told me to keep it some distance from the fire, so that it shouldn't get hot, and I put it in the coolest place I could find. You didn't say when you

Til Eulenspiegel's Merry Pranks

wanted it cooked.'

Meanwhile, the guests had begun to arrive, and the merchant decided that the best thing he could do would be to tell them the whole story. Most of them laughed when they heard it, but the merchant's wife burst out in anger.

'I told you so!' she cried. 'The wretch! Get rid of him at once!'

'I'd better not do that,' said the merchant. 'I am going to Gollai tomorrow, and I shall need him to drive me there. But I promise you that when we are safe back home he shall be dismissed.'

'Thank goodness for that!' said his wife.

Then the master called Eulenspiegel and said: 'Tomorrow I am going with the parson as far as Gollai. See that the coach is ready in the morning, and take care that it is well greased and oiled. I don't want any accidents by the way'

'I will see to it, master,' said the youth. And when all the family was in bed, he proceeded to grease not only the hubs and axles, but also the rest of the coach, inside and out. As a result, when the merchant and parson entered the coach the next morning, and Eulenspiegel suddenly drove off, they both slipped and fell to the floor. They staggered into their seats, but the seats were greasy, too, and with every jolt of the coach they were shot from one end to the other. At last the merchant called out in a great passion:

'Stop! Stop, you idiot! What have you been doing to the coach?'

At that moment a farmer went by, carrying a load of straw in a waggon. The parson and the merchant got out and bought some of the straw. With this they managed to clean the floor and seat of their carriage.

The merchant, looking up from his labours, caught sight of Eulenspiegel's grinning face.

'Go hang yourself, villain!' he shouted, enraged. 'Off to the gallows with you!'

Hearing this, Til Eulenspiegel whipped up the horses and drove

School Times

away at a rapid pace, keeping a sharp lookout for a suitable gallows. At last, he espied one by the roadside. Here he pulled up, got off the driving seat, and began to unharness the horses.

'Now what are you up to?' screamed the merchant.

'This is where you get off, master,' answered Eulenspiegel.

'Where I get off! What do you mean, rascal?'

'Didn't you tell me to drive to the gallows? I thought you wanted me to set you down there.'

The merchant and the priest looked upwards, and saw the gibbet above their heads. The merchant, losing the remains of his patience, cried out: 'Drive straight on in front of you, and don't stop till I tell you to!'

Eulenspiegel did so. Straight in front of them there happened to be a muddy pond, and into this they drove headlong. Of course, the coach got stuck; Eulenspiegel flogged away at the horses, and with a sudden cracking and rending the coach came in two. On went Eulenspiegel with the horses and the front wheels, leaving the merchant and parson stuck in the mud with the hind part of the coach.

The merchant was furious. He leapt down into the mud, waded through it, and began to run after Eulenspiegel. It took him some time to overtake him; when he did, he began to flog the youth soundly, and would no doubt have injured him if the parson had not come up and stopped the quarrel on time. After a good deal of struggling, they managed to fix the parts of the coach together, and the rest of the journey was finished in peace.

'Well,' said the merchant's wife when he returned, 'how did your journey go? How are you feeling now?'

'I'm feeling fine,' said the merchant, 'now I'm back home again.' Then he called Eulenspiegel and said: 'Eat and drink to your heart's content tonight, for you won't get another good meal for many a long day. Tomorrow you quit my house.' And the next morning, before he went out, he said again: 'Eat a good breakfast, take all you want, but don't let me find you here when I come home from church.'

So, while the merchant was at church with all his family, Eulenspiegel got a large waggon, and loaded it with all the goods he could lay hands on: food stores, household furniture, silver plate, ornaments and jewellery. He was just driving away with his load of goods, when he met the merchant coming home from church.

'Ha! My honest cook! What little surprise are you preparing for me now?'

'I'm only doing what I was told to do,' said Eulenspiegel. 'You told me to take all I wanted and quit the house!'

'Leave those things where they are!' commanded the merchant. 'As for you, either you leave the town this instant, or I'll have you whipped out of the place!'

'Just my luck!' grumbled Eulenspiegel. 'I do everything my master orders me to, and yet I can't live in peace!'

But he left the town quickly all the same, and from what I can hear he never showed his face there again.

Ullie's Dream

Heisel Anne Allison

Towards the end of the Second Word War, when the towns and cities of Germany were being reduced to rubble by Allied bombing, a small girl lives on hope that her father will return from the Russian front...

'MAMA,' SHE WHISPERED, 'THAT BOMB was close.'

'Yes, dear,' Mama said. She wrapped her arm around Ullie's shoulders and tried to calm her. 'It's all right. The bombing will be over soon and we'll be fine.'

'But Peter is with his patrol,' Ullie said.

'Don't worry; he'll be all right, too.'

Ullie wanted to believe Mama. She always told her the truth. But it was hard to believe her now.

Ulricka Beck spent most of 1943 and 1944 living in her grandmother's basement with her brother, Peter, her mother and her grandmother, Ursula Heis. It seemed to Ullie that all her life had been spent in this underground room peering through small windows at the top of the walls. But when you're ten years old even six months is a lifetime.

Her brother was in Hitler's Youth Movement. He was able to come and go as he pleased and she resented the hours he spent each day outside drilling with his patrol. She worried when he worked his way home through war-ravaged streets and was irritated because no one ever asked what she thought about the war. She decided it

Ullie's Dream

wasn't much fun being the youngest in the family.

Her village, Mainz Bretzertheim, was being destroyed. Grandmother's house had been spared any serious damage but many of her friends' homes were gone.

Every day the family huddled together in terror as explosions and fires erased their past. They felt lucky to have a roof over their heads.

Ullie was dismayed because her father, Hans, was serving with the Army on the Russian Front. She was eight when her Papa left for the frozen winters in the Ukraine and she dreamed of him almost every night. In her dreams, he was larger than life as he swung her up on his shoulders during their Sunday walks along the Rhine river. She loved Sundays when she could run on the red cobblestones and throw rocks in the Rhine. She could still see his crystal blue eyes laughing back at her as he read stories and helped with her lessons. At night she would stretch out on her narrow cot and think of those wonderful times, her small, serious face glowing in the dark.

Winter, this year, had been the worst time of all. Ullie couldn't seem to stay warm as the snow piled around the tiny windows and food was scarce. She felt sick when she heard Mama tell grandmother they were lucky to catch an occasional stray cat for dinner. She was glad Mama hadn't told her when they were eating cats.

Now, at last, the snow had stopped and the weather was warming a little. Spring would soon be here and Ullie loved spring.

It was dusk when Peter burst through the basement door, gasping for air. Ullie's blue eyes doubled in size when Peter blurted out his news.

'I have heard some of our men are coming home from the Russian Front,' he stammered between breaths. 'The Lieutenant said they should be here within a month.'

Questions tumbled out of Ullie's mouth. 'When will they be here? Is Papa coming home? Is he all right?'

School Times

'Wait,' said Peter. 'I don't know anything else. No one knows anything else except there are many dead.'

In the silence that followed Peter's announcement Ullie stood with her thin arms wrapped tightly around her body. Finally, quiet sobs filled the chilly basement air.

Mama tried to comfort her. I'm sure Papa is all right, Ulricka. You know how lucky he is. You'll see, he'll come home to us safe.'

I'm trying to be strong,' Ullie said. 'But I'm so scared.'

Her body shook and Mama pulled her close. Ullie feared the worst. 'What will I do if Papa doesn't come home? How will I stand it?' she thought.

Cuddled in her Mama's arms Ullie remembered what Papa had said while she listened at the door. 'Must you go?' Mama had asked.

'I don't have a choice. Hitler ordered to close the University and all professors into the Army. I'm being sent to Russia next week. You're strong enough to handle this, Greta, and you must find more strength for the children. Ullie, especially, will need you. When I return, maybe this horrible war will be over and we can rebuild our lives.'

Now she wondered if her strong, handsome Papa would ever come home. As if reading Ullie's mind Mama said, 'He'll come home,' and hugged her tighter.

During the weeks that followed Peter's news, Ullie struggled to keep her spirits up. When the bombing stopped at night she was allowed to go outside and explore what was left of their destroyed garden. Before the war her grandmother's house and garden were famous in all of Bretzenheim. The once green lawn was now brown lumps of dirt and the large goldfish pool was empty except for trash. Ullie smiled in the dark remembering the beautiful flowers behind the front gate and the big heads of lettuce her grandmother used to grow.

The kiosk across the street was blown up recently and shrapnel riveted the walls of the little house the family now shared. Ullie was secretly excited by the war and wanted to find a piece of the metal from the bomb. She was making her way around the house when she heard a strange noise.

Frightened, she let out a small squeak. She pressed her body flat against the wall and peered around the corner of the house. Her hand covered her mouth and she trembled as she watched a shadow making its way up the road. It was a big man and he was limping. Sliding along the wall she made her way to the basement door and slipped inside.

'Mama, there is someone outside,' she whispered, as if he could hear. 'He is so big and he looks funny in the dark. I think he's hurt.'

They turned off the lights, peeked outside and saw their neighbour, Helmut Bachman, walking slowly past.

'He was with Papa,' her mother said. 'Maybe he knows something.'

Ullie was out of the door running toward Helmut Bachman before her mother could warn her to be careful.

Helmut Bachman was startled by Ullie's sudden appearance.

She was just as surprised by his appearance. He was seriously injured and his once beautiful uniform was in rags. The bandage wrapped around his shoulder was stained with blood and his foot looked awful.

'Helmut Bachman,' cried Ullie, her face staring up at him, 'have you seen Papa? Do you know where he is? Did he come home with you?'

By now the entire Beck family was staring at his mutilated body. Tears tumbled down Ullie's cheeks while she watched her father's friend struggled to tell them what he knew.

'Ullie, I saw your Papa in the hospital. He was injured and the troops found him nearly frozen in the snow. I don't know anything else. I didn't see him on the train but it was crowded.' Looking at her mother he said, I'm sorry I can't give you better news. Now I must

School Times

go to my family.' He turned and slowly started up the street.

'My Papa is not dead,' Ullie shouted at the figure disappearing into the darkness.

'Ullie, stop that. Come inside,' said Mama. 'Helmut Bachman has told us everything he can.'

With a heavy heart, Mama tried to coax Ullie to the basement door.

'Come, let's go in the house.'

'No. My papa is not dead,' shouted Ullie. 'He's coming home. I see him.'

'Ullie, you don't see him. There is no one in the street,' Mama said, grabbing her shoulders. 'Come inside.'

Ullie wriggled from her grasp and bolted down the moonless road.

'No,' she screamed. 'Papa is not dead. He's coming home to me,' and she ran faster into the darkness.

She never heard Mama's cries pleading for her to come back. Her eyes were riveted on the figure, only she saw, in the distance. His broad shoulders were straight and he walked proudly up the dark street.

She hesitated only a second when she saw the left sleeve of his tattered jacket hanging free while the right one swung with his stride.

The large, strong man swept down with one arm and lifted his daughter off the ground. Tears streamed down his wide face as he hugged her to him tightly. Ullie covered Papa's face with kisses and wrapped her arms around his neck.

'I knew you would not die,' she whispered as they walked toward the rest of the family.

Ullie's dreams had come true. Her Papa was back home. In her ten-year-old world she knew everything would be all right after all.

Dreams of Elephants

Thomas Palakeel

FOR A MIDDLE-CLASS BOY growing up in the 1960s, in a Roman Catholic pocket of the southern Indian state of Kerala, the most acceptable ambition was to become a missionary. My mother was probably thinking that I might even become a bishop. Once, as I was pretending to be asleep, I overheard her whisper to my sisters that I was the most innocent of her boys, that my face itself was the manifestation of innocence, that I really had the Great Call, the Vocation.

But I had decided to become an elephant hunter. The autobiography of a walrus-mustached elephant hunter named Ittan Mathewkutty being serialized in the Sunday paper, had such an impact on me that I started dreaming about dropping out of school and going away with a mahout. When my cousin ran away from home I envied him and shocked everyone at home by describing him as a brave boy.

Once I followed a domestic elephant a few miles and finally worked up enough courage to talk to the mahout about my interest in becoming an elephant hunter like Ittan Mathewkutty. The sinister-looking mahout smiled as he chewed betel nuts, exhibiting all his teeth dripping with red betel juice, but he did not say a word. Except for his periodic commands to the huge animal walking ahead of us with about a ton of palm leaves tucked in between its tusks (its dinner), the whole atmosphere was quiet.

About an hour later, we reached a river that was drying up very early in the summer. The mahout asked the elephant to step into the water. The animal turned around and looked at me with its tiny eyes, laid down the palm leaves, and obediently entered the pool. The water level rose and soaked my feet. I backed up. The mahout also stepped into the water. With a coconut husk, he started scrubbing the endless black mass submerged in the greenish water. I observed him studiously, admiring his hard work; soon he started wiping sweat off his forehead. When my legs ached, I perched on the low-branch of a jackfruit tree and watched the mahout make the elephant turn sides and scrub the other side.

After the elephant was bathed, the mahout himself took a dip in an upper corner of the pool. When the majestic black elephant, with pink spots on its massive earlobes and humungous trunk, and the long, well-rounded, sword-like tusks shining after the wash, emerged from the pool, I applauded in great joy. I knew that I would certainly dedicate my life for one such indescribable beauty.

This time the mahout looked up to the tree I was perched on and smiled: 'What do you think?' 'My dear tusker,' I said.

'This one belongs to the gods.' The mahout meant that the elephant was the property of a Hindu temple.

'I want to become a mahout,' I said.

'Didn't you want to become an elephant hunter a while ago?' the man laughed.

'That's when I grow up,' I said.

'These boys!' he said, 'Go home and study'

'Could you give me an elephant hair?' I asked.

Now the mahout was buckling up the huge metal chain elephants wear around their backs. I loved the deep clanging of these chains, and I heard this sound often in my dreams.

'An elephant hair to make a ring for my mother,' I added.

Dreams of Elephants

The mahout smiled again, unsheathed his fierce-looking knife with his right hand, grabbed the elephant's moving tail with his left, and cut out a long hair from the end of the tail. He handed it to me with a smile. 'Go home and do your homework.'

As I stood there gazing at the miraculous, strong, wire like elephant hair resting on my palms, the mahout walked ahead, uttering those mysterious commands which the noble animal obeyed like a child. And I ran home with the elephant's hair. The elephant's hair had provoked serious discussions in our family about my divine future. My sisters confirmed that I wouldn't settle for anything less than the immortality of the walrus-mustached elephant hunter. And I was banned from reading the autobiography of Ittan Mathewkutty and the Mandrake the Magician cartoons.

The censorship was painful, especially because I was deprived of heroes to identify with and to mould a fanciful world around. The previous several years' heroes, Neil Armstrong, Edwin Aldrin, and Michael Collins, were not in the newspapers any more. Man's historic landing on the moon had become just another date in history. However, I could always go back to my Apollo II album that I had created with black and white pictures cut out of newspapers and magazines.

My favorite ones were the three family photos: I admired the Armstrong-Aldrin-Collins boys and girls, revered the waves, and deified the great astronaut trio in those pictures. The picture of Edwin Aldrin descending the ladder of the lunar module never failed to intrigue me. There was another newspaper picture of the trio in Bombay a few months after the landing on the moon, and this particular picture made me impatient about my boyhood. I wished to grow up fast.

The tension about me at home was aggravated one night when I did not return from my father's village store, where I was sent to pick up groceries. On my way back, I met a gang of Hindu boys who were going to a temple festival. Even though Christian boys were not welcomed to enter the Hindu temple, my good friends invited me to join them. Though I was taught in catechism classes horrible things about the myriads of Hindu gods, I decided to follow my friends to the festival.

When I returned after midnight, my father asked my mother not to feed me. The punishment was first of all for going to the Hindu temple, and then for returning home late.

Ashamed by the punishment, I went to bed, but my mind was filled with the vivid scenes of the festival: decorated elephants bearing Hindu icons wrapped in red silk, a dozen drummers orchestrating the loudest ritual tunes, conch blowers, the Brahman priests, two old men fanning the deity atop the elephant with a pair of exquisite fans made of feathers, women dressed in golden-brocaded saris leading the procession with oil lamps, and thousands watching their lord pass by with attentive devotion.

In the morning, I declared my fasting protest to the whole family and hid myself in the attic. I was seriously planning to starve myself to death. I had read in my textbook how Gandhi did this and brought the British to their knees. When I didn't go down to the kitchen, turning down both breakfast and lunch, my mother came to the attic door late in the afternoon and said that she accepted defeat.

I clambered down the ladder without speaking a word. My sisters were all watching this from different vantage points. Lunch was ready for me on the table.

'This child hasn't eaten anything for the last twenty-four hours,' my mother said as she served more curries on my plate. After I had eaten a few rice balls dipped in the curry, my mother asked my sister Molly to bring a banana for me as a dessert.

Molly went up the ladder and screamed, staring into the attic where only a bare banana stalk was hanging from the roof beam:

'Mom, he ate all the bananas!'

Everyone in the household laughed and rushed to the dining room to see the new Gandhi. My mother laughed, too. I didn't. When my father came home from the store that night, my mother told him about my fasting and about the two dozen bananas that had disappeared from the attic. My father also laughed, but he said that if I was let out freely into the village anymore, I might end up like a filthy mahout: low class, crude, immoral, eventually poor.

When everyone talked about my mahout-heroes in such abysmally low terms, it made me wonder what could be more adventurous than becoming the absolute master of an elephant.

In the tempestuous monsoon at the end of that summer, our century-old school building collapsed. In the new school year, about two-thirds of the students were to be accommodated in the Catholic parish hall and the rest in the small auditorium at the Hindu temple.

I learned that my parents were planning to send me to an English school. I hoped to avoid going to the school by winning my mother's confidence. I would bribe her with a secret gift: a ring made of fine gold, threaded around the elephant's hair. But my parents wanted to save me from class degradation and elephant worship that threatened my future. Soon I left the safety of Thidanad and my Malayalam world and was sent to the English school.

– Reprinted from the Christian Science Monitor Boston

The Mountain

Charles Mungoshi

WE STARTED FOR THE BUS station at the first cockcrow that morning. It was the time of the death of the moon and very dark along the mountain path that would take us through the old village, across the mountain to the bus station beyond. A distance of five miles, uphill most of the way.

The mountain that lay directly in our path was shaped like a question mark. I liked to think of our path as a question, marked by the mountain. It was a dangerous way, Chemai had said, but I said that it was the shortest and quickest if we were to catch the 5 a.m. bus. I could see that he did not like it but he said nothing more, to avoid an early quarrel.

We were of the same age although I bossed him because I was in Form Two while he had gone only as far as Standard Two. He had to stop because his father, who didn't believe in school anyway, said he could not get the money to send Chemai to a boarding school. We had grown up together and had become great friends, but now I tolerated him only for old time's sake and because there was no one within miles who could be friends with me, someone who had gone to school, I mean. So I let Chemai think we were still great friends, although, I found him tedious and I preferred to be alone most of the time, reading or dreaming. It is sad when you have grown up together but I could not help it. He knew so little and was afraid of so many things and talked and believed so much rot and superstition that I could not be his friend without catching his fever.

From home the path ran along the edge of a gully. It was a deep, steep gully but we knew our way. The gully was black now and in the darkness the path along its rim was whitish. You never know how much you notice things on a path: rocks, sticking-out roots of trees, holes, etc., until you walk that path at night. Then your feet grow eyes and you skirt and jump obstacles as easily as if it were broad daylight.

On our right, away into the distance, was bush and short grass and boulders and other smaller gullies and low hills that we could not see clearly. Ahead of us dawn was coming up beyond the mountain but it would be long, not till almost sunrise, before the people in the old village saw the light. The mountain cast a deep shadow over the village.

We walked along in silence but I knew Chemai was afraid all the time and very angry with me. He kept looking warily over his shoulder and stopping now and then to listen and say, 'What's that?' although there was nothing. The night was perfectly still except for the cocks crowing behind us or way ahead of us in the old village. We barely made any noise in our rubber-soled canvas shoes. It can be irritating when someone you are walking with goes on talking when you don't want to listen to, especially at night. There was nothing to be afraid of but he behaved as if there was. And then he began to talk about the Spirit of the Mountain.

He was talking of the legendary gold mine (although I didn't believe in it, really) that the Europeans had failed to drill on top of the mountain. The mountain had been the home of the ruling ancestors of this land and the gold was supposed to be theirs. No stranger could touch it, the people said. We had heard these things when we were children but Chemai told them as if I were a stranger, as if I knew nothing at all. And to annoy him, because he was annoying me, I said.

School Times

'Oh, fibs. That's all lies.'

He started as if I had said something I would be sorry for. 'But there are the holes and shallow pits that they dug to prove it.' 'Who dug?'

'The Europeans. They wanted to have the gold but the Spirit would not let them have it.'

'They found no gold. That's why they left,' I said.

'If you climb the mountain you will see the holes, the iron ropes and iron girders that they abandoned when the Spirit of the Mountain broke them and filled the holes with rocks as soon as they were dug.'

'Who told you all this?' I asked. I knew no one ever went on top of the mountain, especially on that part of it where these things were supposed to be.

'All the people say so.'

'They lie.'

'Oh, what's wrong with you? You know it's true but just because you have been to school you think you know better.'

I knew he was angry now. I said, 'And don't I, though? All these things are just in your head. You like being afraid and you create all sorts of horrors to make your life exciting.'

'Nobody has to listen to you. These things happen whether you say so or not.'

'Nothing happens but fear in your head.'

'Do you argue with me?' his voice had gathered fury.

'Remember I grew up here too,' I said.

'But you haven't seen the things I have seen on that mountain.'

'What have you seen?'

'Don't talk so loud.' He lowered his voice and went on, 'Sometimes you hear drums beating up there and cows lowing and the cattle-driving whistles of the herd-boys. Sometimes, early in the hot morning sun, you see rice spread out to dry on the rocks. And

The Mountain

you hear women laughing at a washing place on a river but you cannot see them.'

'I don't believe it,' I said. The darkness seemed to thicken and I could not see the path clearly. 'I don't believe it,' I said again and then I thought how funny it would be if the mountain suddenly broke into wild drumbeats now. It was crazy, of course, but for no apparent reason at all I remembered the childhood fear of pointing at a grave lest your hand got cut off.

It was silly, but walking at night is unnerving. I didn't mind it when I was a kid because I always had father with me then. But when you are alone a bush may appear to move and you must stop to make sure it is only a bush. You are not quite sure of where you are at night. You see too many things and all of them dark so you don't know what these things are, for they have no voice. They will neither move nor talk and so you are afraid. It is then you want someone older, like father, to take care of things for you. There are many things that must be left unsaid at night but Chemai kept on talking of them. Of course the teachers said this was all nonsense. I wished it were so easy to say so here as at school or in your heart as in your mouth. But it would not help us to show Chemai that I was frightened too. However, I had to shut him up. 'Can't you ever stop your yapping?'

We had crossed a sort of low hill and were dropping slightly but immediately we were climbing sharply towards the mountain. It loomed dark ahead of us like a sleeping animal. We could only see its jagged outline against the softening eastern sky. Chemai was walking so lightly that I constantly looked back to see if he was there. We walked in silence for some time but as I kept looking back to see whether he was there I asked him about the road that I had heard was going to be constructed across the mountain.

'They tried but they could not make it,' he said. 'Why couldn't they?'

'Their instruments wouldn't work on the mountain.'

'But I heard that the mountain was too steep and there were too many sharp, short turns.'

'No. Their instruments filled up with water.'

'But they are going to build it,' I said. 'They are going to make that road and then the drums are going to stop beating.' He kept quiet and I went on talking. It was maddening. Now that I wanted to talk he kept quiet. I said, 'As soon as they set straight what's bothering them they are going to make that road.' I waited for him to answer but he didn't. I looked over my shoulder. Satisfied, I continued. And think how nice and simple it's going to be when the road is made. A bus will be able to get to us in the village. Nobody will have to carry things on their heads to the station any more. There will be a goods store and a butchery and everybody will get tea and sugar and your drums won't bother anyone. They shall be silenced forever.'

Just as listening to someone talking can be tiring, so talking to someone who, for all you know, may not be listening, can also be tiring. I shut up angrily.

We left the bush and short grass and were now passing under some tall dark trees that touched above our heads. We were on a stretch of level ground. We couldn't see the path here because there were so many dead leaves all over the ground and no broken grass to mark the way.

I couldn't say why but there was a lightness in my tongue; it grew heavy in my mouth and head, and I felt a tingling in my belly. I could hear Chemai breathing lightly, with that lightness that is a great effort to suppress a scream; almost a catching of the breath as when you have just entered a room and you don't want anyone in the room to know that you are about.

Suddenly through the dark trees, a warm wind hit us in the face as if someone had breathed on us. My belly tightened but I did not stop. I heard Chemai hold his breath and gasp, 'We have just passed a witch.' I wanted to scream at him to stop it but I had not the voice. Then we came out of the trees and were in the bush and short grass, climbing again. I released breath slowly. It was much lighter here, and cooler.

Much later, I said, 'That was a bad place.'

Chemai said, 'That's where my father met witches eating human bones, riding on their husbands.'

'Oh, you and your . . .' He had suddenly grabbed me by the arm. He said nothing. Instinctively I looked behind us. There was a black goat following us.

I don't know why but I laughed. Then, after I had laughed, I felt sick. I expected the sky to come shattering itself round my ears but nothing happened, except Chemai's fear-agitated hand on my shoulder.

'Why shouldn't I laugh?' I asked. 'I'm not afraid of a goat.'

Chemai held me tighter. He was shaking me as if he had paralysis agitans. I grew sicker. But I did not fall down. We pushed on, climbing now, not steeply, but enough to make us sweat, towards the old village, into the shadow of the mountain whose outline had now become sharper. It was lighter than when we had started, probably third cockcrow, but it was still dark enough to make us sweat with fear.

'You have insulted her,' Chemai said accusingly.

I said nothing. It was no use pretending I didn't know what I was doing. I knew these goats. Lost spirits. Because I had laughed at it, it would follow me wherever I went. It would eat with me, bathe with me, sleep with me. It would behave in every way as if I were its friend or, better still, its husband. It was a goat in body but a human being in spirit. We had seen these goats, as children, grazing peacefully on the hills and there was nothing in them to tell they were wandering spirits. It wasn't until someone laughed at them or said something nasty to them that they would file in a most ungoatlike manner after whoever had insulted them. And then, when this happened, it needed the elders and much medicine brewing to appease them, to make them go away.

We walked on very quietly now. We came into the open near the old village school. The path would pass below the old church, and a mile or less on we would enter the village.

There would be no question of our proceeding beyond the village this morning, while it was still dark. I didn't care whether we caught the 5 o'clock bus or not. I just did not have the strength to cross the mountain before the sun came up.

Also I had to see my grandmother about our companion.

'Let's wait for daylight in the village,' I told Chemai. I saw his head bob vigorously in the dark.

My grandmother lived in the old village. She had refused to accompany us and many other people of the village when we moved further west to be near water. She said this was home — our home — and she would die here and be buried here and anyone who died in the family would be brought back to the old village to be buried. She had had a long argument with my father but she had been firm. I did not like the old village nor grandmother Jape because both of them reminded me of my childhood and the many nightmares in which I dreamt of nothing but the mountain having moved and buried us under it. And then I would scream out and wake upand the first thing I would smell was grandmother Jape's smoke-dyed, lice-infested blankets that were coarse and warmly itchy and very uncomfortable to sleep in.

I rarely paid her any visits now, and I wouldn't have stopped to say hello were it not for the goat and my fear to cross the mountain in the dark. She would know what to do.

We were now below the church.

Suddenly the church gave me an idea. It had two doors each in opposite walls. We would try to leave the goat in the church. It was a further insult but I felt the risk was worth taking.

The Mountain

When I told Chemai he said he did not like it.

'I shall try it anyway,' I said.

'She will not stay. She will get out.'

We went up the path leading to the church door. We went in. The goat followed. I shouted, 'To the other door, quick!'

Chemai rushed for the opposite door. The goat followed him but stopped suddenly when the door banged to in its face. I slipped through this other door and shut that one behind me too.

Free. We ran for the village a mile up the hill. Grandmother's hut was near the centre of the village. I knew my way about and in a short time we were knocking on her door, each time looking back over our shoulders to see whether the goat had escaped. I had to say, 'It's me, Nharo,' before grandmother would open for us. 'Many things walk in the night with evil in their hearts,' she had once told me.

'What brings you here in the middle of the night?' 'Nothing. We are going to the bus. We want to go to Umtali.'

'To the bus at this hour? Are you mad? You must be . . .' She was looking behind us and I knew our friend had escaped. Quickly we slipped through the door, but the goat followed us into the hut.

Without saying anything grandmother was already busy with her medicine pots. And suddenly, safe and warm, I felt that the goat was harmless. It was just a wronged friend and would go away when paid. I looked at it. It was* a small she-goat, spotless black. In the dim fire glow of grandmother's hut it looked almost sad.

Grandmother was eating medicines and Chemai was watching her intently. I felt safe. Somebody who knew was taking care of things at last. It is a comforting feeling to have someone who knows take care of those things you don't know.

Snails

Dibakar Barua

A Powerful story from Bangladesh. . . .

It's 1971. A CIVIL WAR has been spreading, like eczema, from the cities of East Pakistan to its villages. Thirty miles south of the port city of Chittagong, a chill has come down on Manpur village where men and boys of different religions gather after dusk in secret, segregated societies.

Ajoy, a boy of seventeen, is sitting in a Buddhist cabal in his cousin Tunu's house. Tunu is adding to the evening's collection of rumours. 'The Hindus are getting it,' he says. 'Muslims are taking away their furniture, radios, clothes. Suren Mitra, a Hindu businessman, has killed two looters with a gun. He is trying to escape to India through the mountain trek from Bandarban.'

'But listen,' says another, 'the Muslims may not get him, but the Kukis in the Hill Tracts . . .'

He doesn't finish the sentence. Everyone there knows about the naked Kukis. They yawn. Their voices become sleepy. As the night grows still, they hear the boom boom of a Pakistani warship shelling the Chittagong port.

At his home, Ajoy's mother kneels in front of a framed picture of the Buddha hanging on the plastered mud wall of their downstairs bedroom. She is reciting Pali sutras. A candle flickers in front of the Buddha, and shadows dance around his orange halo. Ajoy lights an incense stick and kneels, too. His brother Bijan hasn't come home for two nights. A clerk in the Telephone and Telegraph office in Chittagong, Bijan walks every morning to the Arakan highway to catch a bus, and returns in the evening.

'Why wouldn't he send a message?' their mother asks. 'Maybe he can't,' says Ajoy. 'The T&CT office is a high security zone.'

'You mean they're surrounded by the troops?' their mother's voice has a tremor.

Ajoy regrets his invention. To his mother, Pakistani troops are bloody butchers. They unzip pedestrians and kill all uncircumcised males.

'Go to sleep, Ma. If Bijan doesn't come home tomorrow, I'll go and see and ask Yusuf Malek.'

Yusuf Malek, who also works in the T&T office, helped Bijan get the job after Bijan's father, a high school teacher, died four years ago. Yusuf can afford two residences and comes to the village on weekends.

To Ajoy's mother, Yusuf Malek and Karim Haq are the only good Muslims of Manpur. The others! She'd rather not talk about them. Karim Haq is a landless peasant who tills her few acres of rice paddies for half shares. For a month in the harvest season, he carries bundles of paddy to her house and thrashes them from morning to night. He has become almost a family member.

It was Karim Haq who brought the news of his father's death to Ajoy. Bijan had just graduated from high school and the two brothers made a trip to Cox's bazaar, a long and wide sand beach on the Bay of Bengal, sixty miles to the south. They stayed in a hilltop temple, listening to the ocean at night, and walked to the shore every day.

Less than an inch below the wet sand near the water lay masses of tiny snails, fingernail whorls with coloured dots — red, purple, yellow, blue.

'Cowries!' Bijan cried.

Ajoy had played a cowrie game with his brother, throwing four polished shells on the floor. If all four landed upside down, the rule was to grab them before the other could.

'These aren't cowries,' he said.

'Well, they're smooth. They have dots,' Bijan said. 'They're certainly not your big drab tree snails.'

'You're right. They're pretty,' Ajoy said.

Then ignoring Bijan's call to ride the waves, Ajoy spent a long time picking those shiny round things and washing the wet sand off them before filling the pockets of his shorts.

'There must be hundreds of thousands of these,' Bijan said, exasperated.

'Millions.'

'Billions.'

Ajoy was thinking of what came after billions when Bijan pointed to Karim Haq walking toward them. He looked so solemn that the brothers laughed. Saying nothing, Karim put his arms across their shoulders, holding the two brothers in an embrace.

Before leaving, Ajoy took the snails out of his pockets and threw them into the ocean.

Bijan hasn't come home for a full week. The mother sleepwalks at night, talking to herself, groping around the closed-in porch like a blind woman. The sight startles Ajoy. He knows his mother to be a perennial sufferer who can steel herself against adversity with a philosophical outlook on life. '*Anicca, dukkha, anatta,*' she has often repeated in conversation, chanting the Pali words like a mantra. When his aunts come to her, complaining or crying, maybe because a cow has died, 'Oh, *anicca, dukkha, anatta,*' his mother says: impermanence, suffering, non-self.

Yes, she is very different from his illiterate aunts. When his father was carried beyond the Rauli Pond for cremation, the widowed aunts filled the afternoon air with ear-splitting wails, scaring crows out of mango trees, but also reassuring Ajoy that his father was not unlamented. His mother, during this time, managed only an occasional whimper, the kind she had emitted when accusing his father of unwise shopping if he had brought home a soft fish that had to be cooked with a massive amount of chili paste. It was as if by dying, his father, with his usual lack of worldly savvy had presented her with yet another irritating domestic problem.

Ajoy never knew his father well. A balding man with a shadowy presence, a domed silence even in the classroom, he used to read the newspaper while his students wrote compositions. Ajoy often wondered how, with what strange innocence or affectation, his father had named his first two children, both girls, with sonorous Bengali nouns — *Swadhinata and Shalinata*, Freedom and Courtesy. These children died in infancy.

It was his mother who told Ajoy about his sisters and prompted him to think about life and suffering. As a pious Buddhist she wanted to be delivered from both.

'Grief's worse than death,' she once said, reminiscing about the death of her children. 'The dead are the lucky ones.'

She told him how hard she had tried to save her two daughters, and how each had died within a month of birth. 'My body was poisonous, I suppose, and so was my milk,' she had said. 'When Bijan came and lived beyond his sixth month, that was a cork on my grief.'

Ajoy stops his sleeping mother's hand from emptying a glass of water on her head.

'It's hot,' she says, waking up. 'Did he come home?' 'No, Ma.'

She sits down on the earthen floor and looks at him, her eyes red with tears. 'Oh son, we'll never see him again.'

Ajoy wants to cry out. Don't weep, mother. I'm here now, your able son. I'll wipe away your tears, and free you from grief, from luckless husbands, and a doomed country. I'll give you peace and happiness. He wants to say all this but only hears a hum in his head, an indistinct sound of crickets or is it an idling car engine? He wonders what remains when that stops.

Like his mother, Ajoy doesn't have the theatricality of grief that his aunts display on demand. He hasn't told her what he learned four days ago from Yusuf Malek. After Malek came home, Ajoy had crossed the road that divided their side of the village from the Muslim side, and stood in front of Malek's door. Chickens clucked in the yard. A young woman passing by drew her veil and ran inside. Yusuf Malek, a man of fifty with a grizzled goatee and a skull cap came to the door.

'Come in my nephew,' he said, courting a convention by which all villagers claimed kinship with each other by a tacit agreement.

'Mother's very worried,' Ajoy said. 'Did something happen at the office?'

Malek made him sit on a cushion, and called out to a sour looking boy to fetch tea. His silence made Ajoy nervous.

'Inshallah' (God willing), he said at last, 'no harm has come to him.'

'Chacha, what's happened?'

'Well, I'm not sure…See…'

Ajoy could guess what was coming and waited for the revelation, listening to Yusuf Malek's digressions. Malek talked about the tight security around the T&T office, and how security guards were replaced by army troops, how all Bengalis were brothers, how the freedom movement was misguided to begin with, giving scope to the worst elements in society and so on. His monotone merged into a hum in Ajoy's head like winter mists descending on Rauli Pond.

Someone in the T&T office, no doubt a member of a pro-Pakistani Muslim League, bore a grudge against Bijan. When the army came, he made a report that Bijan was a Bangladesh supporter.

Snails

The army picked up Bijan for questioning, and drove him to the Cantonment among the Jalalabad Hills.

Ajoy remembers being on a bus once on Kaptai Highway when someone said, 'That's the Cantonment!' pointing toward a row of hills. One hill had a carved black and white crescent over two swords. The barracks couldn't be seen, only fields of rye and rice dancing green and yellow in the sun. Now Ajoy's anxious visions keep mingling with that pastoral beauty. The undulating rice and a brother's blood, the bright rye blossoms and a darkening face, dispersing, along the gray-green hills, like torn petals.

In the days after seeing Malek, Ajoy has thought of the hills, the wind blowing over them in solitude. He has wandered from pond to pond, from one rice field to another, avoiding the night meetings, avoiding his mother. His mother has begun spending days in the monastery, talking to the village monk or praying. The fields are bare now, cracked into stubbled fissures. Ajoy wishes to see rainstorms, an early monsoon, a steady downpour, vibrating their tin roof with a deep bass, filling the pond surfaces with air bubbles, suffusing all his senses. He feels trapped by his own stillness.

An outward stillness also hums on the Rauli Pond. Ajoy walks round and round on its grassy banks, feeling prickles under his feet and in the air. Ants and goldbugs swarm unseen; dragonflies whir transparent wings on the water; a giant banyan broods in the northeast corner, its tapering leaves displaying intricate veins which shimmer in the sun.

A small geometrical figure pops up at a distance, floating toward the village, hovering above the winding dusty path made by numerous footfalls after the harvest. As it nears, Ajoy makes out the wiry thin body of Karim Haq as a vertical line in its middle. He's carrying bunches of cut bamboo arranged in a triangle, his shoulders holding up the middle on a pole. Ahh, so he goes to the mountains for bamboos when the tilling season is over. Ajoy knows so little about the world of work and men! He lets Karim Haq pass by.

The compact darkness, aloud with crickets, can only be pierced by a needle, so the expression goes. Ajoy can't see even his hands, as he makes his way to Karim's hut that night. Through a checkered bamboo door, Ajoy sees a kerosene lamp flicker in an empty room. Karim and his wife Hena-bibi are in their outdoor kitchen. Karim sits with his back against a bamboo wall, and his wife is blowing through a hollow, polished piece of bamboo, trying to get a fire from the embers in her oven. 'Cooking again?'

They are startled. Then they smile and offer Ajoy a wicker mat.

'No, bhai,' says Hena-bibi, 'we already ate rice. But your brother here wants popcorn.'

'What brings you here at this hour, *bhaijan*?' Karim asks.

Karim calls Ajoy bhaijan — little brother — with almost a bashful affection. Suddenly Ajoy feels very unsure. Why indeed has he come to Karim and Hena-bibi after their children have gone to bed, when they are enjoying a rare moment of leisure and privacy?

'How's Aunt,' asks Hena-bibi, sensing his discomfort.

Ajoy tells them what he hasn't told his mother, or cousin Tunu, or anyone from the village. He maintains a matter-of-fact tone.

'Hai Allah, ya Allah,' Karim says, shaking his head from side to side. Hena-bibi seems struck with muteness.

'But why haven't you told your mother?' Karim asks, his voice rising in disbelief.

'Yes,' says Hena-bibi, finding her voice again. 'She should know. She should know before we do.'

I'm going to tell her tonight,' says Ajoy.

'Do you want me to come along?' Karim asks. 'You? No, that won't be . . .'

They remain quiet for a moment. Then Ajoy speaks again. 'Tell me, Karim-bhai, why do you Muslims do this?'

'Do what?'

'Loot Hindu villages, spy on freedom fighters, become finks for the Pak army.'

'Bhaijan, you shouldn't believe everything you hear in your gossip nights.'

'Bijan's missing. That's not gossip.'

'That's the government. What can you do about that?' Karim said. 'Bhaijan, we're simple people,' he said again after a brief silence. 'We try to do good to everyone.'

'I'm sorry. I'll go home now.'

In the darkness that has dissipated slightly, Ajoy hears a faint rat-tat-tat of machine gun fire. The army must have driven out the resistance from Chittagong to some place further south, nearer, probably to Kalurghat Bridge across the Karnaphuli River, a major road link between the city and the country. The nightly shelling of Chittagong has ended.

Ajoy walks to the Rauli Pond, a still and darkened silver form. He takes off his shorts. The darkness and the night air touch him. The water is sweet, with a faint aroma of mud, and lilies blooming on scattered pads. Ajoy wades carefully through the thin bamboo poles dug into the edges of the pond to, prevent clandestine fishing. Then he propels himself with vigorous backstrokes toward the silvery middle, watching the silhouette of the big banyan tree move as he moves.

A waning half-moon is up, showing only the head of the Buddhist hare. In one of his many incarnations, Gautama was a hare, and gave up his life to feed a lost hungry man. To honour this great sacrifice, the gods put his image on the moon. Death is an illusion. One only changes forms. *O, Ananda, untold are your births and deaths, like grains of sand reaching the horizons.* This is a Pali sutra his mother recites. Millions of colourful whorls on the Cox's bazaar sand. They are ourselves, strewn across time, tinted, and necessarily broken.

Ajoy is overcome with dread. His mother is wrong. Grief is not worse than death. Life is, the endless, inexplicable life. How sensible now seems the wild lament of his widowed aunts. What else is there to do but lament? Lament the losses, the deaths, the war. Lament the pond, the wind, the fields of grain, the whirring dragonflies, and dancing rye flowers. Lament the snails of Cox's bazaar.

Flashlights and voices bring Ajoy back to himself.

'Bhaijan,' he hears Karim shout. 'Bhaijan, you'll catch a fever.'

'Ajoy,' Cousin Tunu cries, 'Ajoy, come out of the water.'

One by one they gather on the north bank, waving flashlights and hurricane lamps.

Splashing water and trembling a little, Ajoy leaves the warm pond and clambers up to the dry land, naked.

– Short Story International (Student Series)

Charge!

Stephen Crane

THE BRIGADE WAS HALTED IN the fringe of a grove. The men crouched among the trees and pointed their restless guns out at the fields. They tried to look beyond the smoke.

Out of this haze they could see running men. Some shouted information and gestured as they hurried.

The men of the new regiment watched and listened eagerly, while their tongues ran on in gossip of the battle. They mouthed rumours that had flown like birds out of the unknown.

'They say Perry has been driven in with big loss.'

'Yes, Carrott went t' th' hospital. He said he was sick. That smart lieutenant is commanding 'GJ' Company. The boys say they won't be under Carrott no more if they all have t' desert. They all knew he was a—'

'Hannises' batt'ry is took.'

'It ain't either. I saw Hannises' batt'ry off on th' left not more'n fifteen minutes ago.'

'Well—'

'Th' general, he ses he is goin' t' take th' hull command of th' 304th when we go it eh action, an' then he ses we'll do sech fighth as never another one reg'ment done.'

'They say we're catchin' it over on th' left. They say th' enemy driv' our line inteh a devil of a swamp an' took Hannises' batt'ry'

'No sech thing. Hannises' batt'ry was 'long here 'bout a minute ago.'

'That young Hasbrouck, he makes a good off'cer. He ain't afraid 'f nothin'.'

'I met one of th' 148th Maine boys, an' he ses his brigade fit th' hull rebel army fer four hours over on th' turnpike road an' killed about five thousand of 'em. He ses one more sech fight as that an' th' war'll be over.'

'Bill wasn't scared either. No, sir! It wasn't that. Bill ain't getting scared easy. He was jest mad, that's what he was. When that feller trod on his hand, he stood up an' sed that he was willin' give his hand t' his country but he'd be dumbed if he was goin' t' have every dumb bushwhacker in th' kentry walkin' 'round on it. So he went t' th' hospital disregardless of th' fight. Three fingers was crunched. Th' dern doctor wanted t' amputate 'em an' Bill, he raised a heluva row, I hear. He's a funny feller.'

The din in front swelled to a tremendous chorus. The youth and his fellows were frozen to silence. They could see a flag that tossed in the smoke angrily. Near it were the blurred and agitated forms of troops. There came a turbulent stream of men across the fields. A battery changing position at a frantic gallop scattered the stragglers right and left.

A shell screaming like a storm banshee went over the huddled heads of the reserves. It landed in the grove, and, exploding redly, flung the brown earth. There was a little shower of pine needles.

Bullets began to whistle among the branches and nip at the trees. Twigs and leaves came sailing down. It was as if a thousand axes, wee and invisible, were being wielded. Many of the men were constantly dodging and ducking their heads.

The lieutenant of the youth's company was shot in the hand. He began to swear so wondrously, that a nervous laugh went along the regimental line. The officer's profanity sounded conventional. It relieved the tightened senses of the new men. It was as if he had hit his fingers with a tack-hammer at home.

He held the wounded member carefully away from his side, so that the blood would not drip upon his trousers.

Charge!

The captain of the company tucking his sword under his arm, produced a handkerchief and began to bind with it the lieutenant's wound. And they disputed as to how the binding should be done.

The battle-flag in the distance jerked about madly. It seemed to be struggling to free itself from an agony. The billowing smoke was filled with horizontal flashes.

Men running swiftly emerged from it. They grew in numbers until it was seen that the whole command was fleeing. The flag suddenly sank down as if dying. Its motion as it fell was a gesture of despair.

Wild yells came from behind the walls of smoke. A sketch in grey and red dissolved into a mob-like body of men who galloped like wild horses.

The veteran regiments on the right and left of the 304th immediately began to jeer. With the passionate song of the bullets and the banshee shrieks of shells were mingled loud catcalls and bits of facetious advice concerning places of safety.

But the new regiment was breathless with horror.

'Gawd! Saunders's got crushed!' whispered the man at the youth's elbow. They shrank back and crouched as if compelled to await a flood.

The youth shot a swift glance along the blue ranks of the regiment. The profiles were motionless, carven; and afterward he remembered that the colour-sergeant was standing with his legs apart, as if he expected to be pushed to the ground.

The following throng went whirling around the flank. Here and there were officers carried along on the stream like exasperated chips. They were striking about them with their swords and with their left fists, punching every head they could reach. They cursed like highwaymen.

A mounted officer displayed the furious anger of a spoiled child. He raged with his head, his arms, and his legs.

School Times

Another, the commander of the brigade, was galloping about bawling. His hat was gone, and his clothes were awry. He resembled a man who has come from bed to go to a fire. The hoofs of his horse often threatened the heads of the running men, but they scampered with singular fortune. In this rush they were apparently all deaf and blind. They heeded not the largest and longest of the oaths that were thrown at them from all directions.

Frequently over this tumult could be heard the grim jokes of the critical veterans; but the retreating men apparently were not even conscious of the presence of an audience.

The battle reflection that shone for an instant in the faces of the mad current made the youth feel that forceful hands from heaven would not have been able to have held him in place if he could have got intelligent control of his legs.

There was an appalling imprint upon these faces. The struggle in the smoke had pictured an exaggeration of itself on the bleached cheeks and in the eyes wild with one desire.

The sight of this stampede exerted a flood-like force that seemed able to drag sticks and stones and men from the ground. The youth from the reserves had to hold on. They grew pale and firm, and red and quaking.

The youth achieved one little thought in the midst of this chaos. The composite monster, which had caused the other troops to flee had not then appeared. He resolved to get a view of it, and then, he thought he might very likely run better than the best of them.

There were moments of waiting. The youth thought of the village street at home before the arrival of the circus parade on a day in the spring. He remembered how he had stood, a small, boy, full of thrill, prepared to follow the dingy lady upon the white horse, or the band in its faded chariot. He saw the yellow road, the lines of expectant people, and the sober houses. He particularly remembered an old fellow who used to sit upon a cracker-box in front of the store and

Charge!

feign to despise such exhibitions. A thousand details of colour and form surged in his mind. The old fellow upon the cracker-box appeared in middle prominence.

Someone cried, 'Here they come!'

There was rustling and muttering among the men. They displayed a feverish desire to have every possible cartridge ready in their hands. The boxes were pulled around into various positions, and adjusted with great care. It was as if seven hundred new bonnets were being tried on.

The tall soldier, having prepared his rifle, produced a red handkerchief of some kind. He was engaged in knitting it about his throat with exquisite attention to its position, when the cry was repeated up and down the line in a muffled roar of sound.

'Here they come! Here they come!' Gun-locks clicked.

Across the smoke-infested fields came a brown swarm of running men who were giving shrill yells. They came on, stooping and swinging their rifles at all angles. A flag, tilted forward, sped near the front.

As he caught sight of them, the youth was momentarily startled by a thought that perhaps his gun was not loaded. He stood trying to rally his faltering intellect so that he might recollect the moment when he had loaded, but he could not.

A hatless general pulled his dripping horse to a stand near the colonel of the 304th. He shook his fist in the other's face. 'You've got to hold 'em back!' he shouted savagely; 'you've got to hold 'em back!'

In his agitation the colonel began to stammer. A-all r-right, general, all right, by Gawd! We-we'll do our—we-we'll d-d-do—do our best, general.' The general made a passionate gesture and galloped away. The colonel, perchance to relieve his feelings, began to scold like a wet parrot. The youth, turning swiftly to make sure that the rear was unmolested, saw the commander regarding his men in a highly resentful manner, as if he regretted above everything his association with them.

The man at the youth's elbow was mumbling, as if to himself, 'Oh, we're in for it now! Oh, we're in for it now!'

The captain of the company had been pacing excitedly to and fro in the rear. He coaxed in schoolmistress fashion, as to a congregation of boys with primers. His talk was an endless repetition. 'Reserve your fire, boys — don't shoot till I tell you — save your fire — wait till they get close up — don't be damned fools —'

Perspiration streamed down the youth's face, which was soiled like that of a weeping urchin. He frequently, with a nervous movement, wiped his eyes with his coat-sleeve. His mouth was still a little open.

He got one glance at the foe-swarming field in front of him, and instantly ceased to debate the question of his piece being loaded. Before he was ready to begin — before he had announced to himself that he was about to fight — he threw the obedient, well-balanced rifle into position, and fired a first wild shot. He was working at his weapon like an automatic affair.

He suddenly lost concern for himself, and forgot to look at a menacing fate. He became not a man but a member. He felt that something of which he was a part — a regiment, an army, a cause, or a country - was in a crisis. He was welded into a common personality which was dominated by a single desire. For some moments he could not flee — no more than a little finger can commit a revolution from a hand.

If he had thought the regiment was about to be annihilated, perhaps he could have amputated himself from it. But its noise gave him assurance. The regiment was like a firework that, once ignited, proceeds superior to circumstances until its blazing vitality fades. It wheezed and banged with a mighty power. He pictured the ground before it was strewn with the discomfited.

There was a consciousness always of the presence of his comrades about him. He felt the subtle battle made brotherhood more potent even than the cause for which they were fighting. It has a mysterious fraternity born of the smoke, and danger of death.

He was at a task. He was like a carpenter who has made many boxes, making still another box, only there was furious haste in his movements. He, in his thought, was careering off in other places, even as the carpenter who, as he works, whistles and thinks of his friend or his enemy, his home or a saloon. And these jolted dreams were never perfect to him afterward, but remained a mass of blurred shapes.

Presently he began to feel the effects of the war atmosphere — a bliss wing sweat, a sensation that his eyeballs were about to crack like hot stones. A burning roar filled his ears.

Following this came a red rage. He developed the acute exasperation of a pestered animal, a well-meaning cow worried by dogs. He had a mad feeling against his rifle, which could only be used against one life at a time. He wished to rush forward and strangle with his fingers. He craved a power that would enable him to make a world-sweeping gesture and brush all back. His impotency appeared to him, and made his rage into that of a driven beast.

Buried in the smoke of many rifles, his anger was directed not so much against the men whom he knew were rushing toward him, as against the swirling battle phantoms which were choking him, stuffing their smoke robes down his parched throat. He fought frantically for respite for his senses, for air, as a babe being smothered attacks the deadly blankets.

There was a blare of heated rage mingled with a certain expression of intentness on all faces. Many of the men were making low-toned noises with their mouths, and these subdued cheers, snarls, imprecations, prayers, made a wild, barbaric song that went as an undercurrent of sound, strange and chant-like, with the resounding chords of the war march. The man at the youth's elbow was babbling.

School Times

In it there was something soft and tender, like the monologue of a babe. The tall soldier was swearing in a loud voice. From his lips came a black procession of curious oaths. Suddenly, another broke out in a querulous way, like a man who has mislaid his hat. 'Well, why don't they support us? Why don't they send supports? Do they think—'

The youth in his battle-sleep heard this as one who dozes hears.

There was a singular absence of heroic poses. The men, bending and surging in their haste and rage, were in every impossible attitude. The steel ramrods clanked and clanged with incessant din as the men pounded them furiously into the hot rifle-barrels. The flaps of the cartridge-boxes were all unfastened, and bobbed idiotically with each movement. The rifles, once loaded, were jerked to the shoulder and fired without apparent aim into the smoke or at one of the blurred and shifting forms which upon the field before the regiment had been growing larger and larger, like puppets under a magician's hand.

The officers, at their intervals, rearward, neglected to stand in picturesque attitudes. They were bobbing to and fro, roaring directions and encouragements. The dimensions of their howls were extraordinary. They expended their lungs with prodigal wills. And often they nearly stood upon their heads in their anxiety to observe the enemy on the other side of the tumbling smoke.

The lieutenant of the youth's company had encountered a soldier who had fled screaming at the first volley of his comrades. Behind the lines these two were acting a little isolated scene.

The man was blubbering and staring with sheep-like eyes at the lieutenant, who had seized him by the collar and was pommeling him. He drove him back into the ranks with many blows. The soldier went mechanically, dully with his animal-like eyes upon the officer. Perhaps there was to him a divinity expressed in the voice of the other — stern, hard, with no reflection of fear in it. He tried to reload his gun, but his shaking hands prevented. The lieutenant was obliged to assist him.

The men dropped here and there like bundles. The captain of the youth's company had been killed in an early part of the action. His body lay stretched out in the position of a tired man resting, but upon his face there was an astonished and sorrowful look, as if he thought some friend had done him an ill turn. The babbling man was grazed by a shot that made the blood stream widely down his face. He clapped both hands to his head. 'Oh!' he said, and ran. Another grunted suddenly as if he had been struck by a club in the stomach. He sat down and gazed ruefully. In his eyes there was mute, indefinite reproach. Farther up the line, a man standing behind a tree, had had his knee-joint splintered by a ball. Immediately he had dropped his rifle and gripped the tree with both arms. And there he remained, clinging desperately and crying for assistance, that he might withdraw his hold upon the tree.

At last an exultant yell went along the quivering line. The firing dwindled from an uproar to a last vindictive popping. As the smoke slowly eddied away, the youth saw that the charge had been repulsed. The enemy were scattered into reluctant groups. He saw a man climb to the top of the fence, straddle the rail and fire a parting shot. The waves had receded, leaving bits of dark debris upon the ground.

Some in the regiment began to whoop frenziedly. Many were silent. Apparently, they were trying to contemplate themselves.

After the fever had left his veins, the youth thought that at last he was going to suffocate. He became aware of the foul atmosphere in which he had been struggling. He was grimy and dripping like a labourer in a foundry. He grasped his canteen and took a long swallow of the warmed water.

A sentence with variations went up and down the line. 'Well, we've helt'em back. We've helt'em back; derned if we haven't.' The men said it blissfully, leering at each other with dirty smiles.

The youth turned to look behind him and off to the right and off to the left. He experienced the joy of a man who at last finds leisure in which to look about him.

Under foot there were a few ghastly forms motionless. They lay twisted in fantastic contortions. Arms were bent and heads were turned in incredible ways. It seemed that the dead men must have fallen from some great height to get into such positions. They looked to be dumped out upon the ground from the sky.

From a position in the rear of the grove a battery was throwing shells over it. The flash of the guns startled the youth at first. He thought they were aimed directly at him. Through the trees he watched the black figures of the gunners as they worked swiftly and intently: their labour seemed a complicated thing. He wondered how they could remember its formula in the midst of confusion.

The guns squatted in a row like savage chiefs. They argued with abrupt violence. It was a grim powwow. Their busy servants ran hither and thither.

A small procession of wounded men were going drearily toward the rear. It was a flow of blood from the torn body of the brigade.

To the right and to the left were the dark lines of other troops. Far in front he thought he could see lighter masses protruding in points from the forest. They were suggestive of unnumbered thousands.

Once he saw a tiny battery go dashing along the line of the horizon. The tiny riders were beating the tiny horses.

From a sloping hill came the sound of cheerings and clashes. Smoke welled slowly through the leaves.

Batteries were speaking with thunderous oratorical effort. Here and there were flags, the red in the stripes dominating. They splashed bits of warm colour upon the dark lines of troops.

The youth felt the old thrill at the sight of the emblem. They were like beautiful birds strangely undaunted in a storm.

Charge!

As he listened to the din from the hillside, to a deep pulsating thunder that came from afar to the left, and to the lesser clamours which came from many directions, it occurred to him that they were fighting, too, over there, and over there, and over there. Heretofore, he had supposed that all the battle was directly under his nose.

As he gazed around him, the youth felt a flash of astonishment at the blue, pure sky and the sun gleaming on the trees and fields. It was surprising that nature had gone tranquilly on with her golden process in the midst of so much devilment.

– Stephen Crane: *The Red Badge of Courage (1895).*

Boy Among the Writers

David Garnett

JOSEPH CONRAD PAID MANY VISITS to the Cearne. On one of the first occasions, when I was five years old, I asked him why the first mate of a ship was always a bad man and the second mate good. I don't know what stories I had been reading which had put this into my head, but I remember Conrad's laughing and confusing me by saying: 'For many years I was a first mate myself.'

It was next morning that we made friends. There was a jolly wind, and it was washing day I was alone with Conrad, and suddenly he was making me a sailing boat. The sail was a clean sheet tied at the top corners to a clothes-prop and hoisted with some spare clothesline over one of the clothes-posts. The sail was lashed at the foot, and I held the sheet fastened to the other corner in one hand while it bellied and pulled. The green grass heaved in waves, the sail filled and tugged, our speed was terrific. Alterations were made and the rig perfected and when, an hour later, Edward[1] came out looking for his guest, he found him sitting in our big clothes basket steering the boat and giving me orders to take in or let out the sail.

I met Conrad again when my mother and I were staying with Ford and Elsie Hueffer at Aldington knoll, a little Kentish farmhouse looking out over Romney Marsh. Ford was at his most lovable and

---

[1] Edward Garnett, the author's father, most gifted of publisher's advisers; his occupation, 'the discovery of talent in unknown writers.'

genial. There was a stream running through the garden, and Ford had installed a little wooden water-wheel with two brightly-painted wooden puppets who seemed to be working very hard as they bent down and straightened up incessantly. Really the water turned the wheel and the wheel made them move up and down, bending their backs.

He later adopted the name of Ford Madox Ford, and some people regard him as a great novelist. At the time I first remember him, Ford was a very young man, tall and Germanic in appearance, with a pink and white complexion, pale, rather prominent, blue eyes and a beard which I referred to, when we first met, as 'hay on his face', in spite of the fact that I had been well broken in to beards by those of Sergey Stepniak and Peter Kropotkin.

Ford married Elsie Martindale, whom he first met at school when they were both small children. Elsie was tall, high-breasted and dark, with a bold eye and a rich, high colour, like a ripe nectarine. She dressed in richly-coloured garments of the William Morris style and wore earrings and a great amber necklace, and I, at the age of five, was at once greatly attracted by her. Without undue hesitation I proposed marriage, and when Elsie pointed out that Ford was an obstacle, I said cheerfully that it would be a good thing if he died soon. Although Ford was at once informed of my intention of superseding him, he bore no rancor and was a most charming entertainer of my youth. He would suddenly squat and then bound after me like a gigantic frog. He could twitch one ear without moving the other — dreadful but fascinating accomplishment. He would also tell me stories, just as he told everyone else stories — but I do not think I ever believed that anything he said was true.

The next time we saw the Hueffers they had moved from Aldington Knoll to Winchelsea, and we stayed in lodgings next door to them. The South African War was drawing to a close; it was perhaps the late summer of 1901. There was a flower show in

School Times

Winchelsea the day after we arrived, and troops paraded in dark green uniforms with felt hats turned up on one side, and the military band played 'The Last Rose of Summer' and other airs through a long, hot and dusty afternoon. I had been given a Browinie Kodak. A few days later we went over in a hired wagonette to Rye and called upon Henry James, whom we found dressed in an extremely tight-fitting pair of knickerbockers and an equally exiguous jacket of black-and-white checks. When he came out with us and showed us Rye he wore a very tight-fitting cap on his vast head. In this costume, he was kind enough to pose for me, and the photograph I took came out perfectly. Lamb House astonished me by its tidiness, the beautiful furniture in the drawing-room, the perfection of a passage and the beautiful garden. Ford, tall and fresh-coloured, smiling and showing his rabbit teeth, enjoyed himself, patronizing my parents on one side and James on the other. Perhaps my parents were aware of the possibility that they were being thrust upon the Master by Ford. If they were right in that suspicion! I am duly grateful to Ford, for I should not otherwise have had tea with Henry James in Lamb House. He walked back a little way with us, and we said goodbye to him on the edge of Rye and walked down from the high ground to where our conveyance was waiting.

Then a new visitor came to the Cearne to win my heart. He was W.H. Hudson, a very tall lean man with red-brown eyes which could flare up with anger or amusement and then die down again. He had a short beard, a twisted aquiline nose that had been broken in some fight in South America, a wide forehead and a curiously flat top to his head, and big bony hands. His voice, gentle and deep in tone, became suddenly rasping and fierce when Edward teased him — which he was always doing. Hudson wore an old-fashioned tail-coat made of some pepper-and-salt or brown tweed with pockets in the tails and a stand-up, stiff white collar to his shirt.

His first visit was in winter, but he came again in the spring and summer following. One spring morning, I went out with him into the woods; the majority of the trees were still bare; only the hawthorn and a few forward sprays of beech were covered with leaves. I was astonished because he continually identified birds by their song, and the song of a missel-thrush led us to a missel-thrush's nest in the fork of a young oak. Standing silently in the warm spring sunshine, listening to the wild and rapturous song of the storm-cock, I felt very close to my tall companion.

I told him that I had seen a frog unlike other frogs. Together we went down across the fields below the Cearne to Trevereux pond where there was a nightingale singing, and there Hudson found my 'other frog' which was in reality a kind of toad — a natterjack.

Hudson's next visit was in the summer. It was a warm balmy night. I had been allowed to stay up and we were all sitting in the front porch, when the sound of a nightjar calling, not far off, aroused Hudson.

We followed him silently to the top of the garden, and there in the next field, we hid under some bushes. I was under a gorse bush and had to keep motionless and silent in spite of its prickles.

Then Hudson began calling to the birds, imitating their whirring rattle perfectly. Soon a nightjar answered him, then after a pause Hudson called again, and so it went on, bird and man calling to each other until in the end, the birds — for there were more than one — came to investigate. There was a sudden clap of wings over our heads and a dark shadowy bird whirled away, then another warning clap of wings as another swept over and discovered the impostor. After that it was no good, and we got up, brushed the leaves and prickles off our clothes and walked back, delighted by our sudden contact with the nightjars.

There were glow-worms that night in the grass, and it was then that I told Hudson that I had seen a phosphorescent light like a chain of green beads and, on lighting a match, had found a centipede.

School Times

Once again my observation was confirmed and I won praise.

Another visitor who came about that time was a short, thickset man of great energy and determined character — Hilaire Belloc. During his visits, he seldom listened to anything my parents said and never stopped talking; he sat up late drinking wine and talking to my father and then got up much too early the next morning. But he not only had energy within himself; he imparted it to all of us, and for a short time after his visit, the defeatist atmosphere that my father's philosophy imparted to me was blown away.

Nothing in the world could be more poisonous to a boy than that philosophy. For Edward usually spoke as though he believed that the finest talents were never recognized; the most sensitive and charming people were ruined and oppressed by the coarse and brutal; that the survival of the fittest meant that ruthlessness, brutality, ugliness and stupidity triumphed and exterminated the beautiful, the sensitive and the gifted. And I was, of course, axiomatically to regard myself as one of the doomed minority. This philosophy, which might have had some truth in it had it been propounded by the Last of the Mohicans, was grotesque nonsense. But I did not realize what nonsense it was until I was nearly twenty, when one day I said to myself:

> For hundreds of thousands of years the weakly and the stupid have died; the ugly girls have gone unwed and the beautiful ones been chosen for the mothers of the race by the strongest and most intelligent men. I and everyone else in the world are the inheritors of the successful: why should I fail now when the blood of the winners in life's race runs through my veins? 1 will not identify myself with a dinosaur.

The memory of Hilaire Belloc's self-confidence faded away; a more lasting memorial of one of his visits was a huge red-and-yellow casserole which he sent to my mother for making *bœuf en daube*.

A far more frequent visitor, and one more congenial to Constance, was a bald serious man of about Edward's age who was to become for many years a close friend of both my parents. He wrote to Constance,[2] in the first instance, because he admired the works of Turgenev, which he had read in her translations, and had himself literary ambitions. Indeed, he had already published a novel and a volume of verses under the Nom de plume of John Sinjohn. He was John Galsworthy, and my parents invited him down to the Cearne and at once adopted the position of his literary mentors.

On his first visit he arrived at the same time as a cat with a kitten. Before departing on holiday with their family, some neighbours, knowing us as cat-lovers, brought us their half-wild cat which had newly kittened. Two days later, I found our palsied dog, Puppsie, bouncing in on the cat and the kitten in the big room. I rushed forward and grabbed Puppsie by the collar and dragging him away when the cat sprang at me and, missing my eye, tore my eyebrow asunder. In spite of the pain and one eye being full of blood, I remember looking with awe at the mother cat, which had sprung on to the mantelpiece where she remained with arched back and rigid tail, a spitting fury.

The incident had unhinged her, and she subsequently attacked everyone who entered the room. Jack Galsworthy was scratched, though not so severely as I. At last she was trapped in a basket, and Jack and Constance carried the yowling animal and its kitten back to their home, where they liberated them in a woodshed, leaving enough provisions for a few days.

Most of the people I had hitherto known would have been flustered or would have reacted in some way to the savage fury of the maddened animal yowling horribly and tearing at the wicker basket. Galsworthy did not react; he remained calmly detached. The

---

[2] Constance Garnett, the author's mother, translator of Turgenev, Tolstoy and Dostoevsky.

cat might have been gently purring for all the emotional response it evoked from him. On one of his early visits the miscreant Puppsie dug up and was dragging a bullock's head into the house, which had been bought many weeks before with some intention of making soup, or feeding the dogs, but which had been buried because bluebottles had laid their eggs on it. These had now reached their greatest development, and maggots were falling from it in legions when my mother and Galsworthy intercepted Puppsie with it in the hall. The literary aspirant did not turn a hair, though the stench would have overpowered most people. He calmly fetched a shovel and a wheelbarrow, conveyed the horrible object to the bottom of the garden, dug a large hole, buried it and then returned to wash his hands carefully and dust his knees with a handkerchief scented with a few drops of eau-de-Cologne.

My chief interest in Galsworthy was that he had stalked deer with a Red Indian guide. He was kind and generous to me, and I rewarded him with the honourable title of Running Elk.

At this stage of his life he was in violent revolt against the Forsyte traditions, and my parents influenced him considerably and not only with literary advice. It was from Edward that Galsworthy drew Bosinney in *The Man of Property* — which gives a certain piquancy to the violent discussion, published in their correspondence, in which Edward assailed Jack for not understanding Bosinney's character, and Bosinney's creator defended himself as best as he might. The reason for Galsworthy's revolt against the Forsyte traditions of his family was that he was in love with Irene (Ada), who was married to his cousin.

For several years, he was deeply unhappy, and all his best work was written at this time. Finally, after his father's death, Jack and Ada resolved to take the decisive step; she left her husband and went to the man she loved. From that moment, Galsworthy was finished as a serious writer. He was happy; he soon became successful and influential, and his natural goodness, his serious desire to assist all the deserving causes near to his heart, ruined his talent. Ada was a sensitive and beautiful woman, with dark hair turning grey and brown eyes, and there was something about her that made me recall bumble bees seen among the velvety petals of dark wallflowers.

Later on, when I was about fifteen, I remember going with Constance and the Galsworthys to a concert. On taking our seats, Ada unpinned her toque and skewered it on to the back of the stall in front with a steel hatpin. Shortly afterwards a gentleman was shown to the seat in front of her. He sat down and leant heavily back in it. There was a violent exclamation and he jumped up. Ada was overwhelmed with concern, which was not dispelled by the gentleman exclaiming: 'Madam, you might have caused my instant death!' and his departing in search of a doctor. During the interval he returned and took his seat in a gingerly manner and, when the concert was over, informed Jack that the doctor thought no vital organ had been touched. I thought the whole incident was extremely comic, and the deep and anxious concern of Jack and Ada added to my amusement, so that I found a good deal of difficulty in suppressing my merriment. My mother also grew very flushed in the face for the same reason. I don't think any of us was able to devote full attention to the music.

I met H.G. Wells for the first time when I was about thirteen or fourteen, when he was brought over two or three times to the Cearne by Sydney Olivier and his daughters. I can see him now as I first saw him, a small figure, bouncing along like a rubber ball between the tall figures of Edward and Sydney, each a head taller than he was, like a boy walking between two men, and all three walking in quite different ways. Edward walked in a long, casual, lurching stride, H.G. Wells positively bounced with ill-suppressed energy, and Olivier strode with aloof dignity, apparently unaware of his companions, to whom he was really listening attentively.

School Times

On another occasion, Wells was brought by the Oliviers' girls alone, and I walked back with them. H.G.'s liveliness and activity dominated all of us, and I remember his instant response to Brynhild's sparkling eyes and flashing smile. But any attraction they felt for each other was suppressed and its expression averted when he played a violent game of rounders after tea.

Wells was, at the time I first saw him, an active figure in the Fabian Society and, when a clash arose between him and the Webbs, my father joined the Society purely in order to vote for Wells and Wells's supporters, when they put up for the Executive Committee. A month later, when wells had been defeated, Edward resigned.

Constance was quite indignant with him over this: he was not a socialist and had no business to pretend to be one merely in order to take part in a fight; but Edward only laughed and left his defence to Maitland, who supported Wells.

H.G. had already caused uneasiness among the conventional owing to his lack of respect for the taboos attaching to sexual desires and, at one moment Lady Olivier forbade her daughters to read *The Sea Lady*. I remember that Brynhild and Margery poured out their indignation to Edward.

But a litde while after I had left university College School, Wells moved to church Row, Hampstead, and the scandal of Annu Veronica broke. The row was prodigious and a considerable portion of it reached my ears. In his *Experiment in Autobiography*, Wells explains that, like many of his characters, the heroine of Ann Veronica was suggested by an actual young woman, who is represented as taking the initiative in sexual relations with a demonstrator in Zoology, a typically Wellsian hero. My memory is that the outraged parents of this young woman attempted to destroy Wells, who became the target for a fantastic social persecution. He was turned out of his club — the Savile — and he and his wife were cut and boycotted, in particular by many socialists who were afraid he would fasten the label of Free Love for ever to the movement.

Shaw, unlike the Webbs, who hated Wells, was one of the few of the leading Fabians to behave with common sense; he urged all concerned to hush up the scandal. But it was too late.

Olivier, though remaining most friendly with Wells, wrote to him at this time a moderate and sensible letter, saying he would not like Wells to be seen in public in the company of his daughters. This letter was the cause of a strange scene at the very height of the scandal. I went one day with Brynhild to an exhibition of paintings in Bond Street. After we had been there some time, she suddenly caught sight of Wells, who was hiding from us behind some pictures on a stand running down the middle of the room. Brynhild called out to him in her clear voice and Wells turned and fled like a rabbit. But he took refuge in a *cul-de-sac*, and Brynhild and I followed and ran him to earth. Her cheeks were scarlet as she held out her hand and her eyes flashed more than ever as she said:

'I won't let you cut me, Mr Wells, so don't ever dare to try to do so again.'

I don't think I ever saw her look lovelier than she did at that moment. She held Wells in talk for five minutes and forced him to look at some of the pictures with us. I could see Wells put into some of the games he made us play. There was rampageous bumping around a table and knocking over of chairs when I had expected to sit around, on my good behavior, listening to highbrow conversation. And then I was dragged into a nursery where a little war was in progress and saw H.G. Wells, in a whirlwind of tactical enthusiasm, ousting his small sons Frank and Gyp from the peaceful enjoyment of their toy soldiers.

I don't think Wells took much notice of me then: but a year or two later, meeting me by the Hampstead Fire Station, opposite the Tube, he said: 'You are following exactly in my footsteps and I suppose later on you'll throw up biology to write novels.' It turned out that he was right in that prophecy as in so many others.

– From *The Golden Echo*

The Old Jug-Dodge has an Unexpected Victim

Talbot Baines Reed

The kind of episode described in this extract is not an unfamiliar one — anyhow, so far as the method is concerned, if not the victim. Other variations of the dodge involve the use of a bag full of flour, actions and so on, suitable to make a shower.

'OH, I DON'T KNOW,' SAID king. 'It's not so bad. I tried to keep a diary once, but I could never find anything to write.'

'Well, I guess Bosher is not hard up in that line,' said Telson, laughing. 'But, I say, we ought to give it to him back somehow.'

'I'll give it to him back pretty hot!' exclaimed Parson. 'I voice we burn the bosh thing.'

'Oh you can't do that. You'd better smuggle it back into his study somehow, King, without his knowing.'

'All serene,' said King, pocketing the book. 'Hallo! Who's this coming?'

As he spoke there was a sound of hurrying footsteps in the passage outside, and immediately afterwards the door opened and revealed none other than the sentimental author of Bosher's diary himself.

Just at present, and luckily for him, he did not appear to be in a sentimental mood; he was a little scared and looked mysterious as he hurriedly stepped into the room and shut the door behind him.

'Look out, I say!' he exclaimed, 'the welchers are coming!'

The magic announcement dispelled in a moment whatever

The Old Jug-Dodge has an Unexpected Victim

resentment may have lurked in the minds of any of the three students on account of the diary. In the presence of a common danger like this, with the common enemy, so to speak, at the very door, they were all friends and brothers at once.

'Where? How do you know?' demanded the three.

'I was looking for a book I had lost,' said Bosher, 'in the Big near our door, and I heard Cusack tell Pilbury to wait till he went and saw if the coast was clear. So they'll be here directly.'

'Jolly lucky you heard them,' said Parson. 'What shall we do, you fellows?'

There was a slight interval for reflection, and then Telson said, 'Fancy the jug-dodge is about the best. They won't be up to it, eh?'

This proposal seemed to meet with general approval, and as time was precious Parson's tin jug, full of water, was forthwith hoisted adroitly over the door, and delicately adjusted with nail and twine so that the opening of the door should be the signal for its tilting over and disgorging its contests on the head of the luckless intruder. It was such an old method of warfare that the conspirators really felt half-ashamed to fall back upon it, only time was short and the enemy might come any moment. As an additional precaution, also, a piece of the twine was stretched across the doorway about three inches from the ground, with the considerate purpose of tripping up the expected visitors. And to complete the preparations, each of the besieged armed himself with an appropriate weapon wherewith to greet the intruders, and thus accoutered they sat down and waited for the event with serene minds.

The event was not long in coming. Before several minutes a stealthy footstep was heard outside, which it was easy to guess belonged to the spy of the attacking party. Parson motioned to the others to be silent, and seated himself at his table, with a book before him, in full view of the keyhole. The little maneuver evidently hold, for the footsteps were heard stealthily hurrying away, and the watchers knew the main body would soon be here.

It seemed no time before the approaching sounds gladdened their expectants ears. The invaders were evidently walking in steps and trying to imitate the heavy walk of some senior, so as to give no suspicion of their purpose.

The besieged smiled knowingly at one another, glanced up at the suspended jug, and then softly rising with their weapons at the 'ready' calmly awaited the assault.

Whoever knew a set of Parrett's juniors caught napping? The welchers would have to be a precious deal more cunning than this if they expected to score off them.

The footsteps advanced and reached the door. There was a brief pause, the handle turned, Parson gave the signal, and next movement — Mr Parrett entered the study!

As he opened the door, the jug overhead, true to its mechanism, tilted forward and launched a deluge of water over the head and shoulders of the ill-starred master, just as he tripped forward over the string and fell prone into the apartment, while at the same instant, accompanied by a loud howl, one sponge, two slippers, and a knotted towel flew into his face and completed his demolition.

What Mr Parrett's reflections may have been during the few seconds which immediately followed, no one ever found out. But, whatever they were, it is safe to say they were as nothing compared with the horror and terror of the youthful malefactors as they looked on and saw what they had done.

With a cry almost piteous in its agony, they rushed towards him and lifted him, dripping and bruised as he was, to his feet, gazing at him with looks of speechless supplication, and feeling crushed with all the guilt of actual murderers.

It spoke volumes for Mr Parrett's self-control that, instead of sitting and gaping foolishly at the scene of the disaster, or instead of suddenly hitting out right and left, as others would have done, he took out his handkerchief and proceeded quietly to dry his face while he collected his scattered thoughts.

At length he said, 'Are these elaborate preparations usually kept up here?'

'Oh no, sir!' cried Parson, in tons of misery. 'Indeed, sir, we never expected you. We expected—'

His speech was cut short by a fresh noise outside - this time the real enemy, who, little guessing what was going on within, halted a moment outside before commencing proceedings. Then, with a simultaneous war-whoop, they half-opened the door, and, without entering themselves, projected into the centre of the room — a bottle! Pilbury and Cusack had not studied natural science for nothing!

The strange, projectile smashed to atoms as it fell, and at the same instant there arose a stench the like of which the nose of Willoughby had never known before.

Mr Parrett and the boys choked and made a dash for the door, but the enemy were hanging on to the handle in full force, and it was at least two minutes before the almost suffocated Parson could gasp, 'Open the door! Do you hear? Mr Parrett's here; let him out.'

'Won't wash, my boy!' cried a mocking voice, 'Won't wash! Wait a bit, we've got another bottle for you when you're quite ready!'

'Let me out, boys!' cried Mr Parrett as well as he could for choking and holding his nose.

'Tell you it won't wash, my boy!' cried the insulting voice outside. 'Try again! Have a little more sulphuretted hydrogen. Jolly stuff, isn't it? Hold on, you fellows, while I chuck it in!'

The idea of another bottle was more than anyone could endure.

Mr Parrett groaned and cleared his throat for another summons, but Parson was before him.

'I say' cried he, in positively piteous tones, 'we give in. I'll apologize, anything — do you hear?'

'Eh - go down on your knees, then,' cried the enemy.

School Times

'I am,' said Parson.

'Is he? The rest of you? Is he on his knees? Both of them?' 'Yes, he is,' cried Bosher. 'Honour bright.' 'Well then, say "I'm a beastly cad, and a funk, and a sneak, and I knuckle under and will never do it any more."'

'I'm a beastly cad,' gasped Parson, choking with shame, anger, and sulphuretted hydrogen, 'and a funk, and a sneak, and I knuckle under and will never do it anymore.'

'Now all the rest of you say it!'

Telson, Bosher, and King obeyed, one after the other. 'Is that all of you?'

'Yes,' said Parson, terrified at the prospect of Mr Parrett having to go through the ordeal. 'Telson, Bosher, King and I are the only boys here.'

'All serene,' cried the jubilant voice outside, 'open the door, you fellows!'

We draw a veil over the scene which followed!

Mr Parrett hurried out of the room the moment the door was open, merely turning to say,

'Come to me all of you at seven tonight!'

And then with his handkerchief still over his mouth he hurried off.

– Talbot Baines Reed: *The Willoughby Captains (1887)*.

Getting Granny's Glasses

Ruskin Bond

Short-listed for the Newberry Prize, this tender story tells of a small boy's long walk in the mountains with his short-sighted Granny . . .

GRANNY COULD HEAR THE DISTANT roar of the river and smell the pine needles beneath her feet, and feel the presence of her grandson, Mani; but she couldn't see the river or the trees; and of her grandson she could only make out his fuzzy hair, and sometimes, when he was very close, his blackberry eyes and the gleam of his teeth when he smiled.

Granny wore a pair of old glasses; she'd been wearing them for well over ten years, but her eyes had grown steadily weaker, and the glasses had grown older and were now scratched and spotted, and there was very little she could see through them. Still, they were better than nothing. Without them, everything was just a topsy-turvy blur.

Of course, Granny knew her way about the house and the fields, and on a clear day she could see the mountains — the mighty Himalayan snow peaks — striding away into the sky; but it was felt by Mani and his father that it was high time Granny had her eyes tested and got herself new glasses.

'Well, you know we can't get them in the village,' said Granny.

Mani said, 'You'll have to go to the eye hospital in Mussoorie. That's the nearest town.'

'But that's a two-day journey,' protested Granny. 'First I'd have to walk to Nain Market, twelve miles at least, spend the night there at your Uncle's place, and then catch a bus for the rest of the journey! You know how I hate buses. And it's ten years since I walked all the way to Mussoorie. That was when I had these glasses made.'

'Well, it's still there,' said Mani's father.

'What is still there?'

'Mussoorie.'

And the eye hospital?'

'That too.'

'Well, my eyes are not too bad, really,' said Granny, looking for excuses. She did not feel like going far from the village; in particular, she did not want to be parted from Mani. He was eleven and quite capable of looking after himself, but Granny had brought him up ever since his mother had died when he was only a year old. She was his *Nani* (maternal grandmother), and had cared for boy and father, and cows and hens and household, all these years, with great energy and devotion.

'I can manage quite well,' she said. As long as I can see what's right in front of me, there's no problem. I know you got a ball in your hand, Mani; please don't bounce it off the cow'

'It's not ball, Granny; it's an apple.'

'Oh, is it?' said Granny recovering quickly from her mistake. 'Never mind, just don't bounce it off the cow. And don't eat too many apples!'

'Now listen,' said Mani's father sternly, 'I know you don't want to go anywhere. But we're not sending you off on your own. I'll take you to Mussoorie.'

And leave Mani here by himself? How could you even think of doing that?'

'Then I'll take you to Mussoorie,' said Mani eagerly. 'We can leave father on his own, can't we? I've been to Mussoorie before, with my school friends. I know where we can stay. But —' He paused a moment and looked doubtfully from his father to his grandmother. 'You wouldn't be able to walk all the way to Nain, would you, Granny?'

'Of course I can walk,' said Granny. 'I may be going blind, but there's nothing wrong with my legs!'

That was true enough. Only day before they'd found Granny in the walnut tree, tossing walnuts, not very accurately, into a large basket on the ground.

'But you're seventy, Granny.'

'What has that got to do with it? Besides, it's downhill to Nain.'

'And uphill coming back.' 'Uphill's easier!' said Granny.

Now that she knew Mani might be accompanying her, she was more than ready to make the journey.

The monsoon rains had begun, and in front of the small stone house a cluster of giant dahlias reared their heads. Mani had seen them growing in Nain and had brought some bulbs home. 'These are big flowers, Granny,' he'd said. 'You'll be able to see them better.'

She could indeed see the dahlias, splashes of red and yellow against the old stone of the cottage walls.

Looking at them now, Granny said, 'While we're in Mussoorie, we'll get some seeds and bulbs. And a new bell for the white cow. And a pullover for your father. And shoes for you. Look, there's nothing much left of the ones you're wearing.'

'Now just a minute,' said Mani's father. Are you going there to get your eyes tested, or are you going on a shopping expedition? I've got only a hundred rupees to spare. You'll have to manage with that.'

'We'll manage,' said Mani. 'We'll sleep at the bus shelter.'

'No, we won't,' said Granny. 'I've got fifty rupees of my own. We'll stay at a hotel!'

Early next morning, in a light drizzle, Granny and Mani set out on the path to Nain.

Mani carried a small bedding-roll on his shoulder; Granny carried a large cloth shopping bag and an umbrella.

School Times

The path went through fields and around the brow of the hill and then began to wind here and there, up and down and around, as though it had a will of its own and no intention of going anywhere in particular. Travellers new to the area often left the path, because they were impatient or in a hurry, and thought there were quicker, better ways of reaching their destinations. Almost immediately they found themselves lost. For it was a wise path and a good path, and had found the right way of crossing the mountains after centuries of trial and error.

'Whenever you feel tired, we'll take a rest,' said Mani.

'We've only just started out,' said Granny. 'We'll rest when you're hungry!'

They walked at a steady pace, without talking too much. A flock of parrots whirled overhead, flashes of red and green against the sombre sky. High in a spruce tree a barbet called monotonously. But there were no other sounds, except for the hiss and gentle patter of the rain.

Mani stopped to pick wild blackberries from a bush. Granny wasn't fond of berries and didn't slacken her pace. Mani had to run to catch up with her. Soon his lips were purple with the juice from the berries.

The rain stopped and the sun came out. Below them, the light green of the fields stood out against the dark green of the forests, and the hills were bathed in golden sunshine.

Mani ran ahead.

'Can you see all right, Granny?' he called.

'I can see the path and I can see your white shirt. That's enough for now.'

'Well, watch out, there are some mules coming down the road.'

Granny stepped aside to allow the mules to pass. They clattered by, the mule-driver urging them on with a romantic song; but the last mule veered toward Granny and appeared to be heading straight for her. Granny saw it just in time. She knew that mules and ponies always preferred going around objects, if they could see what lay ahead of them, so she held out her open umbrella and the mule cantered round it without touching her.

Granny and Mani ate their light meal on the roadside, in the shade of a whispering pine, arid drank from a spring a little further down the path.

By late afternoon, they were directly above Nain. 'We're almost there,' said Mani. 'I can see the temple near Uncle's house.'

'I can't see a thing,' said Granny.

'That's because of the mist. There's a thick mist coming up the valley.'

It started raining heavily as they entered the small market town on the banks of the river. Granny's umbrella was leaking badly. But they were soon drying themselves in Uncle's house, and drinking glasses of hot sweet milky tea.

Mani got up early the next morning and ran down the narrow street to bathe in the river. The swift but shallow mountain river was a tributary of the sacred Ganges, and its waters were held sacred too. As the sun rose, people thronged the steps leading down to the river, to bathe or pray or float flower-offerings downstream.

As Mani dressed, he heard the blare of a bus horn. There was only one bus to Mussoorie. He scampered up the slope, wondering if they'd miss it. But Granny was waiting for him at the bus stop. She had already bought their tickets.

The motor-road followed the course of the river, which thundered a hundred feet below. The bus was old and rickety, and rattled so much that the passengers could barely hear themselves speaking.

One of them was pointing to a spot below, where another bus had gone off the road a few weeks back, resulting in many casualties.

The driver appeared to be unaware of the accident. He drove at some speed, and whenever he went round a bend, everyone in the bus was thrown about. In spite of all the noise and confusion, Granny fell asleep; her head resting against Mani's shoulder.

Suddenly the bus came to a grinding halt. People were thrown forward in their seats. Granny's glasses fell off and had to be retrieved from the folds of someone else's umbrella.

'What's happening?' she asked. 'Have we arrived?'

'No, something is blocking the road,' said Mani.

'It's a landslide!' exclaimed someone, and all the passengers put their heads out of the windows to take a look.

It was a big landslide. Sometime in the night, during the heavy rain, earth and trees and bushes had given way and come crashing down, completely blocking the road. Nor was it over yet. Debris was still falling. Mani saw rocks hurtling down the hill and into the river.

'Not a suitable place for a bus stop,' observed Granny, who couldn't see a thing.

Even as she spoke, a shower of stones and small rocks came clattering down on the roof of the bus. Passengers cried out in alarm. The driver began reversing, as more rocks came crashing down.

'I never did trust motor-roads,' said Granny.

The driver kept backing until they were well away from the landslide. Then everyone tumbled out of the bus. Granny and Mani were the last to get down.

They were told that it would take days to clear the road, and most of the passengers decided to return to Nain with the bus. But a few bold spirits agreed to walk to Mussoorie, taking a shortcut up the mountain which would by-pass the landslide.

'It's only ten miles from here by the footpath,' said one of them. 'A stiff climb, but we can make it by evening.'

Mani looked at Granny. 'Shall we go back?'

'What's ten miles?' said Granny. 'We did that yesterday.'

So they started climbing a narrow path, little more than a goat-track, which went steeply up the mountainside. But there was much

Getting Granny's Glasses

huffing and puffing, and pausing for breath and by the time they got to the top of the mountain Granny and Mani were on their own. They could see a few stragglers far below; the rest had retreated to Nain.

Granny and Mani stood on the summit of the mountain. They had it all to themselves. Their village was hidden by the range to the north. Far below rushed the river. Far above circled a golden eagle.

In the distance, on the next mountain, the houses of Mussoorie were white specks on the dark green hillside.

'Did you bring any food from Uncle's house?' asked Mani.

'Naturally,' said Granny. 'I knew you'd soon be hungry. There are *pakoras* and buns, and peaches from Uncle's garden.'

'Good!' said Mani, forgetting his tiredness. 'We'll eat as we go along. There's no need to stop.'

'Eating or walking?'

'Eating, of course. We'll stop when you're tired, Granny.'

'Oh, I can walk forever,' said Granny, laughing. 'I've been doing it all my life. And one day I'll just walk over the mountains and into the sky But not if it's raining. This umbrella leaks badly.'

Down again they went, and up the next mountain, and over bare windswept hillsides, and up through a dark gloomy deodar forest. And then just as it was getting dark, they saw the lights of Mussoorie twinkling ahead of them.

As they came nearer, the lights increased, until presently they were in a brightly lit bazaar, swallowed up by crowds of shoppers, strollers, tourists and merrymakers. Mussoorie seemed a very jolly sort of place for those who had money to spend. Jostled in the crowd, Granny kept one hand firmly on Mani's shoulder so that she did not lose him.

They asked around for the cheapest hotel. But there were no cheap hotels. So they spent the night in a *dharamsala* adjoining the temple, where other pilgrims had taken shelter.

Next morning, at the eye hospital, they joined a long queue of patient patients. The eye specialist, a portly man in a suit and tie who himself wore glasses, dealt with the patients in a brisk but kind manner. After an hour's wait, Granny's turn came.

The doctor took one horrified look at Granny's glasses and dropped them in a wastebasket. Then he fished them out and placed them on his desk and said, 'On second thought, I think I'll send them to a museum. You should have changed your glasses years ago. They've probably done more harm than good.'

He examined Granny's eyes with a strong light, and said, 'Your eyes are very weak, but you're not going blind. We'll fit you up with a stronger pair of glasses.' Then he placed her in front of a board covered with letters in English and Hindi, large and small, and asked Granny if she could make them out.

'I can't even see the board,' said Granny.

'Well, can you see me?' asked the doctor.

'Some of you,' said Granny.

'I want you to see all of me,' said the doctor, and he balanced a wire frame on Granny's nose and began trying out different lenses.

Suddenly Granny could see much better. She saw the board and the biggest letters on it.

'Can you see me now?' asked the doctor.

'Most of you,' said Granny. And then added, by way of being helpful: 'There's quite a lot of you to see.'

'Thank you,' said the doctor. 'And now turn around and tell me if you can see your grandson.'

Granny turned, and saw Mani clearly for the first time in many years.

'Mani!' she exclaimed, clapping her hands with joy. 'How nice you look! What a fine boy I've brought up! But you do need a haircut. And a wash. And buttons on your shirt. And a new pair of shoes. Come along to the bazaar!'

Getting Granny's Glasses

'First have your new glasses made,' said Mani, laughing. 'Then we'll go for shopping!'

A day later, they were in a bus again, although no one knew how far it would be able to go. Sooner or later they would have to walk.

Granny had a window seat, and Mani sat beside her. He had new shoes and Granny had a new umbrella and they had also bought a thick woolen Tibetan pullover for Mani's father. And seeds and bulbs and a cowbell.

As the bus moved off, Granny looked eagerly out of the window. Each bend in the road opened up new vistas for her, and she could see many things that she hadn't seen for a long time — distant villages, people working in the fields, milkmen on the road, two dogs rushing along beside the bus, monkeys in the trees, and, most wonderful of all, a rainbow in the sky.

She couldn't see perfectly, of course, but she was very pleased with the improvement.

'What a large cow!' she remarked, pointing at a beast grazing on the hillside.

'It's not a cow, Granny' said Mani. 'It's a buffalo.'

Granny was not to be discouraged. Anyway I saw it,' she insisted.

While most of the people on the bus looked weary and bored, Granny continued to gaze out of the window, discovering new sights.

Mani watched for some time and listened to her excited chatter. Then his head began to nod. It dropped against Granny's shoulder, and remained there, comfortably supported. The bus swerved and jolted along the winding mountain road, but Mani was fast asleep.

First published by Julia MacRae,
London, in their Blackbird series
Reprinted in Short Story International

www.ingramcontent.com/pod-product-compliance
Lightning Source LLC
Chambersburg PA
CBHW020802160426
43192CB00006B/413